Under the Burning Sun

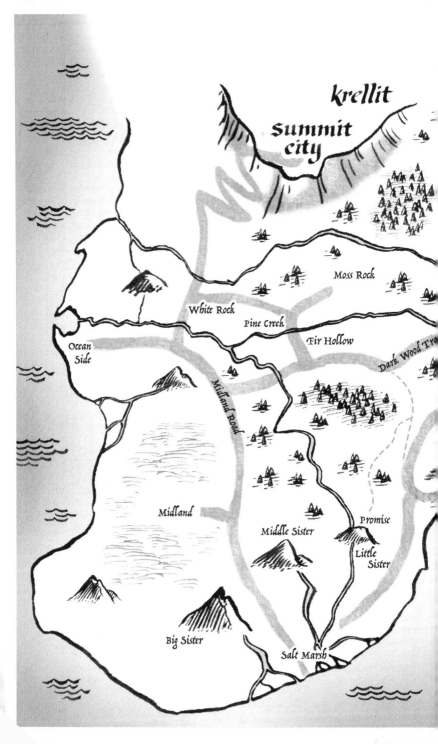

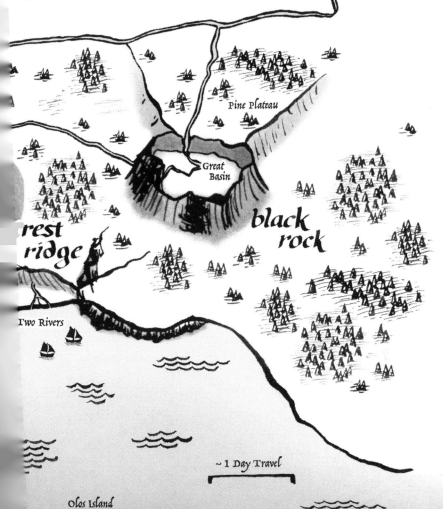

the GReat PRovince

Pine Plateau

Great Basin

crest ridge

black rock

Two Rivers

~ 1 Day Travel

Olos Island

THE FORBIDDEN SCROLLS

by John W Fort

BOOK ONE

———·◇·———

The Shadow of Black Rock

BOOK TWO

———·◇·———

The Other Side of Black Rock

BOOK THREE

———·◇·———

Under the Burning Sun

The Forbidden Scrolls

—·◇·—

John W Fort

Book Three

—·◇·—

Under the Burning Sun

Illustration & cover design by Sydney Six

Pacific Publishing

ISBN-10: 1727166213
ISBN-13: 978-1727166217

To Dr. James Putman
the real Soul Healer in my life

Special thanks to Randy Ingermanson
for your advice and wisdom.

PROLOGUE

----·◇·----

Erif gazed into the small pool, watching the image of a two-wheeled cart riding down a wide dirt road, carrying a young husband and wife and their newborn daughter.

"Now they begin the hard part of their journey," said the snow-bearded spirit next to Erif.

"What came before was not hard?" asked Erif, "Raef living among the Dragon Children in the Great Basin was not hard?"

"He is a Dragon Child himself," said the Great Spirit, "he grew accustomed to it."

"He left them," Erif replied, "remember? He wanted to be free. And why are you arguing against Raef? You are the one who always advocates for him."

"I do advocate for Raef, my Warrior friend. I am merely stating facts."

Erif watched Raef and his wife, Naan, as they traveled south down Midland road. Naan was patting their baby, Nine, consoling her for the dust and noise of the trail.

"He never cut his hair," said Erif.

"Why should he?" asked the Great Spirit, Zul.

"He abandoned his post as Keeper, disgraced his title as leader among his cast. He has no right to wear his hair uncut," Erif replied.

"All Intercessors withhold the razor from their hair," said Zul, "not just the Keepers."

"No Intercessor deserves keep his hair after betraying his village," said Erif.

"So claims the Warrior who has been banished to a deserted island," replied Zul.

Erif became silent—his heart pained at the rebuke.

"This highway is not safe," the ancient spirit said, breaking the silence.

"It is the only road south, they have no choice," said Erif, his voice subdued, "Raef introduced his apprentice, Daz, to the dragon. And Rail kidnapped Daz, taking the greenling to Black Rock to live in the Great Basin. Raef knew he had to leave before anyone found out."

"The villagers know nothing of the Great Basin and the Dragon Children," said Zul.

"It matters not," said Erif, "if the village ever realizes Raef was responsible for the disappearance of Daz, he will be arrested as a traitor. Daz had only thirteen seasons, scarcely a greenling. Though I wish Raef would show bravery and admit his treachery rather than run away."

"Do you not realize that I planned for Raef to escape?" asked the Great Spirit. "That I am the one clouding the villagers' minds so he is not discovered?"

Erif stood and faced the Great Spirit, "Why... why would you help a traitor escape?"

"He seeks a Soul Healer," said Zul, "if Raef is arrested, he cannot find the only one who can free him from the dragon's curse."

"I do not understand why you continue to aide such an errant young man," said Erif.

Erif opened his mouth to continue his case with the ancient spirit, when he saw a group of horsemen closing in on Raef and Naan on the road. They were closing in very rapidly.

"Zul!" cried Erif, "marauders!"

"I see them."

"But, Raef is an Intercessor, he has no training in battle. They will be killed!"

—·◇·—

PART ONE

BEREFT

1

Raef heard rapid hooves closing from behind. He drove his own horse faster, bouncing the cart on the hard road. He leaned toward Naan as the invader approached. A blade sliced through Raef's hair, yanking him back. He pulled free to see a handful of hair swirl away in the wind. Their cart was nearly surrounded.

A loud "thwack" caused Raef to look down and see a thick arrow stuck in the bench next to Naan. Raef pulled the reins to slow his horse. Three horsemen ran past. He looked back and saw two more closing from behind. His infant daughter cried out from Naan's arms.

"Raef, do something!" said Naan.

His mind raced. He was no Warrior. He had never traveled the highways before, much less faced marauders. Their one-horse, two-wheeled cart had no chance escaping the five horsemen. His Intercessor training was of no help whatsoever.

A hooded man veered in front of them. Raef pulled the reins back.

"Don't slow down!" said Naan.

"If we hit him the cart will upset!"

Little Nine was wailing now, adding to the confusion. Naan strapped the Nine to her chest with the baby's blanket. Raef snapped the reins and aimed the cart left, around the man in front. At least the road was a wide and flat.

The lead horseman matched their new course.

Raef tried to speed around him to the right, but it was no use. Hooves thundered all around them.

Raef tossed the reins to Naan and turned in his seat.

"I have never driven a cart!" cried Naan.

Raef ignored his wife, who struggled with the reins. He nearly fell out of the cart rummaging for his sword.

I can die, he thought, *Naan and Nine cannot.*

His hand found the handle of the instrument. He rose to his feet, spinning in a circle and holding out the sword.

It was a small sword, compared to what the marauders carried, but his arms were long. He nearly nicked one man on the neck. Another, who was riding behind them, slowed his horse, as his eyes grew wide. Raef could not hear him, but the man's mouth formed the word, "Intercessor."

"Raef!" yelled his wife.

Four of the marauders fell back. One made a dash forward, grasping one of the sacks in the cart. All five horsemen laughed and made for the brush.

Raef's vision blurred and the sword clattered into the back of the cart. He trembled down onto the bench. The cart was slowing.

"Raef?"

He leaned into his wife as the cart came to a stop. Nine had miraculously stopped crying.

"We were lucky," said Raef, as his vision and strength slowly returned.

"What did they take?" asked Naan.

Raef crawled into the back of the cart, opening sacks to see what was left.

"A day of provisions is missing," he said, "We had better find your Soul Healer soon."

"We will," said Naan, "I am certain of it."

Raef climbed back to the bench and took the reins.

"I am not certain there is such a thing as a Soul Healer."

"Hush!" said Naan, "of course there is. And he will free you from whatever curse you are under."

Raef's lip began to quiver. He hardened his face to make it stop.

"Naan, I was Keeper, remember? I had access to all the sacred scrolls. There are no records of such a healer. I know, I studied every scroll."

Naan looked stoically ahead, not answering her husband. She wrapped Nine a bit tighter then sat up straight.

"Midland is not far now," she said, "I have been there before, with Master Artisan, Matik. The road to Midland will be just ahead."

"Toward the mountains?"

"The road to Midland leads away from the mountains," Naan said.

"But the mountains are where the Soul Healer is said to live!"

"Raef, I know of no city or village closer to these mountains,"

Naan explained, "It is a place to start."

A vaporous reptilian form loomed over Erif, lifting its head a dozen spans above the man. Erif held a long sword, nearly as long as he was tall, his hands low to his left while angling the tip to his right above his head. The smoky conjuration would have to go through the sword to reach him. The dragon's head darted left, then right as Erif held his place. His arms bulged with the effort required to handle such a weapon.

The beast's claw swept toward Erif. The Warrior leapt for it, swinging his blade down, cracking the dragon where talon met paw. The phantom pulled its claw back quickly, curling it under its belly.

"Nicely done," said the ancient being who stood nearby, "it would not expect that."

The dragon lowered its head, looking at its paw.

"It would not do much damage," panted Erif as he lunged up, sinking the sword behind the beast's jaw, "but it gives me a moment to get a better strike!"

The phantom threw back its head, rivulets of inky blood falling around Erif as the sword came loose. Erif stood back and lowered his sword as the beast stepped back. Then the vapor thinned and the image vanished. Zul strode slowly to Erif's side.

"That would set it back a bit," said the old spirit.

"Not for long. Even with all this training I am still just one man. I will need help."

"That is true," said Zul, wrapping his robed arm around the Warrior's bare shoulders.

"Is help going to be hard to find?"

Zul grinned, "So impatient. The future will arrive at its own pace."

"But surely you know who will or will not assist me."

The old bearded spirit chuckled, "Now, where is the fun in telling you that now?"

"Are you saying I am forbidden to know?"

Zul smiled, patting the man's shoulder.

"Trust me, Erif. I am not leading you to failure." Erif smiled.

"Now, let us return to camp and fetch the scroll," said Zul, "It is time to record more of Raef's journey."

Erif's smile faded as he sheathed his sword and strapped it to his stallion's side.

"Another vision?" asked Erif, "you know I dislike watching them."

"As long as you remain banished on this island it is your primary mission."

"I thought my training was my mission."

"That is important, but writing the scrolls is most important of all. The scrolls will save more lives than your sword."

Erif mounted his steed and descended the hill where he had been training. He rode bareback at a gallop to camp, which was near the beach. Zul was already there, waiting by the fire pit. Erif tied the horse, put the sword against some rocks, and opened the box where he kept the scrolls.

"Looks like you need to make more parchments soon," said the spirit.

"Yes," said Erif, "an endless task with all the writing I've done."

Erif pulled a leather cylinder from the box, untied its end, and retracted a tube of parchment. Then he looked to Zul.

"Where to, Great Spirit?"

"There is a clear pool just over this ridge," replied the spirit as he led the way.

Erif followed Zul over a sandy hill into a depression with a circular pool in the center. There was a solitary rock suitable for sitting beside the water. Erif was certain neither the pool nor the rock were there before. He sat on the rock and unrolled the scroll to the place he had left off. He then put a small inkwell he had made from a hollowed stone and a pen he had made from a gull's feather.

The Great Spirit moved his hand in a circle over the pool and the water became clouded and then cleared to reveal Raef and Naan riding their cart between the merchant stalls of Midland.

"It is very noisy here," said Raef.

"Raef, this is a market. What did you expect?"

Raef looked down on his wife, who was smiling. She had always liked commotion. He did not.

Looking in all directions he could not see beyond the rows and rows of merchant tents.

"I have never seen so many merchants in one place," said Raef.

"Midland is a city of trade. Half the city is nothing more than a bazaar. There are merchants from half the Province here selling their wares."

"I was expecting more buildings," said Raef.

"Those are on the far end of the city, where the permanent inhabitants live."

Raef looked down the rows—other than a single barn he could see no wooden structures in the distance. He wondered what other fascinating places Naan had visited before they met.

"We should get started," said Raef, "We can tie up the cart over at that stable. You take Nine and go south. I will go west and see what I can discover."

It was midday when Raef and Naan parted. He asked locals and visiting merchants alike whether anyone had heard of a Soul Healer who lived nearby. No one had heard of such a thing.

Raef eventually found the homes of Midland. These homes were wooden plank structures, not the earthen walled huts of his home village. Even the roofs were mostly wood, rather than grass thatched. Some were quite large, more like lodges than family homes. It was hard to fathom so many with the wealth to live in such a fashion.

He was intimidated to call from the street to summon the owners of such structures, but he gathered his courage and did. Most gave him odd looks when he mentioned "Soul Healer." When the sun began to set he returned to their cart and found Naan waiting.

"I have had no luck," said Raef.

"Neither have I," said Naan, "These people have not been particularly friendly. I had forgotten how cold city dwellers are."

They had last meal using their provisions, then paid the stable master to feed their horse. Raef brought the cart behind the barn and began to rearrange it to sleep in.

"What are ya doing there in your cart, fine sir?" asked a young stable hand who had sauntered up.

"Preparing to sleep," said Raef.

"Here in the stable? Sir, there are inns to sleep in."

"We have no money for that," said Raef, "we can stay here."

"But sir," the greenling responded, "Me thinks ya will not wish to sleep here behind the stables. It be noisy and foul."

"Less noisy than the streets of your city," said Raef.

The greenling craned his neck to look up at Raef.

"We are simple village folk," said Raef, "We do not require much."

The young stable hand scratched his head and looked around in a circle. There was unease in his face.

Naan came to Raef's side and combed her fingers through his hair that ran all down his back.

"My hair," he said to Naan, "I forget it gives me away, even without my Intercessor robe."

He turned back to the greenling, who was now looking meekly up at him.

"I pray I have not offended sir in some way," said the greenling.

"I was an Intercessor, it is true," said Raef, "but I have left my village and am no longer serving such a function. I am not offended to sleep among the horses."

"Ya was? I am not understanding, sir. How can ya be and then not be?"

Raef smiled. One cannot change the class they were born to, unless perhaps a woman by marriage. He could not expect a simple Laborer, much less a greenling, to understand.

"I may look like an Intercessor, with this hair, but I am not."

The greenling looked uneasy, but nodded. Then he turned and vanished into the dusk.

Naan hugged Raef's side and he put his arm around her.

"You will always be an Intercessor to me," she said.

"I feel the Keepers would not agree with you," he said, "I do not know what I am now."

Raef erected a tent over their cart and they entered to sleep. Nine cooed and tugged on Raef's hair, and he smiled down on her. They were nearly asleep when a voice called for them.

Raef poked his head out of the tent to see who it was. The greenling stable hand stood a few paces away, his arms full of hay.

"For you and your missus, sir. Fresh hay for sleeping."

"Thank you," said Raef, reaching out to retrieve

the gift. He was already in his night robe and did not wish to come outside.

"My master asked for ya to have it. He wishes well for ya."

"Then he would be the first in Midland," muttered Raef.

"Raef!" said Naan from inside.

"Tell your master I give him my blessing," said Raef.

"Yes sir," said the greenling, "sleep well."

2

They left Midland City at sunrise, reaching the highway before the sun reached quarter sky. They took the highway south and found it passed between Middle and Big Sister mountains. Though they searched they could find no trace of even a footpath leading toward either mountain. When they had completely passed the mountains they stopped. Other than leaving the cart and walking through the forest on foot Raef realized the only hope of reaching the mountains was to search for a road to the mountains somewhere else.

Raef turned them around and headed back north. He hoped they would not come across marauders again. Raef fumed silently at the wasted suns they had spent searching as they passed the road to Midland again. Naan held Nine and patted Raef's hand reassuringly. He looked at Naan and his heart sank. The likelihood they would find a trail to the mountains was slim. That they would find a Soul Healer was even less.

"Naan, I am going to try, but I have to be honest.

I really do not think I can overcome whatever the
dragon has done to me. I have tried everything
already."

"Zul will help you."

"The Spirit? He does nothing! I have meditated to
him as long as I can remember, done all the ritual
washings, participated in every ceremony. All for
naught. I was a Keeper, for the love of the Province,
and not even that helped."

"Well, I believe he can help."

Raef glanced at her, then looked away and let out
a long sigh.

"I just want you to know that I will probably
never change. It is only fair to tell you. The dragon is
far more powerful than anyone realizes."

Naan's eyes filled with tears, "I refuse not to
believe."

She squeezed his hand as they continued to ride.
Raef did not feel reassured, but he squeezed Naan's
hand back.

They reached Darkwood Trail and followed it east
mid sun next. Early the third sun they passed the trail
to Fir Hollow and continued toward the sunrise. They
had returned to where their journey began. Raef tried
to force down his discouragement. The Three Sisters
Mountains were to the south, where the Soul Healer
was said to live. But between them and the mountains
was a vast forest the cart could not traverse. He
glanced back at their provisions. They only had food
left for two suns. He looked ahead, trying not to think
about…well, about anything.

At sunset it was hard to find a place to camp

between the thick trees and underbrush. The forest was dense here, even beside the road. Next sun the trees seemed to grow taller and the road darker as they traveled. It was easy to see how the road got its name. They found no signs of people by sunset, so they stopped to sleep. They were nearly out of food. The only thing Raef could think of to be grateful for was not running across any more thieves. But then, he realized, why would any thieves be way out here where so few traveled?

Nine was restless and cranky when sunrise came. Raef removed the sleeping tent over the cart, looked up and tried to spot the sun through the trees. Just a flicker of light was visible dancing at the tips of the trees in the east. He had not been up so early since he was an apprentice, many seasons past. It reminded him of getting up to prepare the Ceremonial Lodge for Homage, before even the Keepers arrived.

Raef stared down at his hands and arms, filthy with dirt. He had not performed the ceremonial New Leaf washing since leaving Fir Hollow. He shook his head in silence. Those rituals had done nothing to protect him from Rail as a greenling, and they would do nothing to help him now.

Raef helped Naan and baby Nine up to the bench at the front of the cart, then vaulted up to sit next to them.

"We had better find something by sunset," said Raef, "we will be out of food and we are over a sun's journey back to the nearest village."

"Keep going," said Naan, her face set firmly ahead.

Soon they came across a small trail branching off to the right. Raef stopped the cart. The trail was small and looked rarely used.

"If anyone lives up in these mountains this must be the trail they use," said Raef.

"It is such a small trail," said Naan, "not much more than a foot path. Are you sure the cart will even fit?"

Raef smiled wryly at his wife.

"So, after all these suns, now you begin to doubt?"

"No one said this man lived near a well traveled road," said Raef.

Naan smiled at him. Raef realized it had been many suns since either of them had smiled at all. He patted her hand and jumped to the ground. He walked to the horse, taking its reins and led on foot.

Raef found the path was indeed too narrow. Branches slapped the sides of the cart as it pushed through the brush. Naan wrapped herself around Nine to protect the baby. Dense underbrush lay on both sides, making it difficult to see the path at all.

The woods grew darker and strange animal sounds came from all around. Raef was silent, as was Naan, as they pressed on. Nothing looked familiar, even the plant life was foreign to Raef. The trees were large, with trunks thicker than Raef had ever seen. Emerald strings of moss hung off of everything. As they continued Raef became concerned that they would become stuck. He did not want to continue down a trail that was looking more and more like a poor choice but it was too narrow to turn the cart around.

They stopped for midday meal when the sun was directly overhead. Scarcely enough supplies remained for one meal. After eating they continued on, hoping for a wide spot to turn around. As it began to grow dark they came to another branch in the path. This new branch was smaller, but it appeared to turn directly toward the closest mountain—Little Sister. It was getting too dark to see so they stopped to camp. Naan smiled bravely as she prepared the last of their food.

It was quite cold when the sun went down, especially for late spring. It was odd to hear no sound of human life around them. No distant voices, only sounds from insects and a distant cry from a bobcat. At least Nine seemed to be at peace. She slept nearly until sunrise.

When Naan was feeding Nine next sunrise, Raef stole away and tried to meditate. He was desperate, stuck in the middle of the wilderness with no food. As he sat, eyes closed, he thought he saw an image of an old man's face, far off in the distance. It was fuzzy, not clear. He listened and, though he was not sure, he thought he heard the image speak.

"Follow the path."

"We will only become stuck!" Raef said aloud.

"Follow the path," a faint voice replied.

A memory came to Raef. He was younger, a greenling, walking alone in the Great Basin after sunset. It was dark and pouring rain. Raef saw himself, crying and looking up into the falling rain. He saw himself calling out to Zul for help, but no help came. Not even a voice to comfort him.

Why did you abandon me in Black Rock? Raef wondered. *You knew the dragon was too strong for me. You did not help me then, why should I think you would help me now?*

"Follow the path," said the voice, this time so weak it Raef scarcely heard it.

Raef stood to his feet and opened his eyes, "I am tired of this game!" he said aloud, "Asking for the help of spirits who ignore me!"

The vision was gone. Raef trembled in despair.

"If there is nothing here to help me," Raef said to the void, "I do not wish to continue living. You claim to be the Great Spirit, please just take my life if I am to live as a Dragon Child forever."

Raef waited, but the vision did not return. His face resolute, Raef returned to Naan who was getting into the cart. He silently tied the horse to the cart, took the reins, and walked down the tiny path toward Little Sister.

3

Raef's stomach growled loudly as mid sun approached. He knew Naan was hungry too. He lost the trail now and then but managed to find it again. By three quarter sun the trees began to thin out and Raef could see the sun. He could also see the flattened top of Little Sister directly ahead. No trees grew on the small mountain's flat plateau, while the other two mountains in the distance, much taller, had trees all the way to the peak.

Their cart left the trees and entered low brush, then an open meadow that spread around the base of the mountain.

"I hear voices!" said Naan.

Raef stopped and listened, his heart racing with hope. He heard voices, multiple voices, in the distance. There were voices of men, women, and even younglings—several

A small female youngling burst out of the tall grass in front of them. She stopped, wide eyed, regarding Raef and the cart. She looked to have just seven or eight seasons.

The small one paused. Raef kept still, afraid of frightening her. Then she stood up straighter and looked directly at Raef.

"Do you have any apples?" she asked.

"Do I...what?" asked Raef.

"Apples. Do you got any?" The youngling then began walking in circles, looking into the sky as she talked, "I was wondering because we have no more since before Seasons End and I was asking my daddy but he said the only way to get apples now is from travelers and since I never seen you before you must be a traveler and maybe, I thought, you would have an apple."

The youngling turned to face Raef and scratched her head.

"Well, do you?"

Raef wanted to laugh, but refrained. He bent lower and put on a face he hoped showed kindness, "Could you take us to your father?"

"No," said the youngling.

Raef stood up, shocked at the reply.

"Could you take us to your mother?" asked Naan from behind.

"Of course," said the youngling, "my mother is who watches me when the sun is up."

The youngling turned and began to skip through the grass.

"I can always take you to my mother," the youngling said, "She will be so happy to see you, I know it. We do not have foreigners very often. Well, really, I have never before seen a foreigner..."

Naan smiled at Raef and motioned him to follow.

He pulled the horse and cart and followed the youngling through the meadow. Soon a small circle of huts came into view.

"A village?" asked Raef, "way out here?"

"A bit small for a village," said Naan, "not what I was expecting."

"I thought we'd find some old a hermit living in a hollowed out old tree," said Raef.

Naan laughed. Raef smiled at her, feeling relief set in.

The youngling ran ahead, directly toward a woman who appeared around the side of one of the small huts. The woman smiled broadly as her eyes met Raef's.

"Hello," said the woman, looking directly at Raef.

Raef stepped back, slightly offended by a woman, other than his wife, being so bold to address him directly.

"You look to be travelers," continued the woman, "and tired ones too."

"That we are," said Naan, "We are from Fir Hollow. We have traveled for eight suns trying to find a way to the mountain."

"So many suns away from home," said the woman, shaking her head, "and with a baby too."

Raef stopped the horse as they neared the back of the hut. The woman went straight for the cart and leaned close to Nine, touching her head and cooing.

"I believe I may have heard tell of Fir Hollow," said the woman, "we get very few travelers here in Promise."

"Promise?" asked Raef.

"Yes, our little community. Oh, I am forgetting myself. I am Iris. Welcome to Promise. Come, you look tired. Come and sit."

Naan climbed down from the cart and Iris led her around the hut. Raef tied the horse to a stump and followed. Raef found the two women inside the hut. The little youngling followed close behind, skipping in circles as she walked.

"I will bring you something to drink," said Iris, "If you can stay a bit, you will meet my husband, Siro. He is out gathering today."

Naan looked at Raef. "Gathering what?" she whispered. Raef shrugged.

Iris plopped down two mugs of a drink Raef and Naan could not identify. It was vaguely sweet. The youngling hung on Naan's arm, peering down at little Nine. Iris looked directly at Raef again. He felt himself puff up with offense. Then he shook his head, trying to be grateful, even if the woman did not respect proper custom.

"Yes, we get few visitors here," said Iris, taking a seat next to Naan, "being so far from the big path and all. Oh, it is good to finally have a visitor," she continued, gazing from Raef to Naan, "someday I would like to visit a village. That must be and exciting place to live."

Raef looked at Naan and raised his eyebrows. "Uh, Iris? How many live here in Promise?"

"Oh, yes. Forgot to tell you that. We are perhaps half-a-hundred. Course, a lot of them be younglings. Only seven families in all. And Tren, the bachelor."

Raef smiled at the dialect, "And this adorable

youngling?"

"Oh, yes. Our little Pari. She has eight seasons now."

"This many!" said Pari, holding up eight fingers.

Raef heard his stomach growl loudly.

"Oh my, how thoughtless of me!" said Iris. "Of course you would be hungry. You have missed mid sun meal?"

"Well," Raef began.

"We should not be a burden to you," said Naan.

"Nonsense," said Iris, "you be the first visitors come in two seasons. That is nearly nobility to the likes of us."

"Stay and eat!" called little Pari, jumping and throwing her arms in the air.

"Iris," said Raef, "we will be okay until last meal."

"No, no, I have some pottage left over I can heat up. Pari, go fetch some bread from Glenna."

The youngling darted out the door as Iris hooked a kettle over the central fire pit and stirred the coals to life. Iris worked over the pot, singing a tune Raef did not know. Soon Pari returned with a loaf, handing it to her mother. The youngling promptly returned to Naan's size, peering down at the baby.

"What is the baby's name?" asked Pari.

"We named her 'Nine,'" answered Naan.

Pari scrunched up her face, wrinkling her nose, then she looked up and Naan.

"Why is your baby called 'Nine'"?

Raef grinned.

"Well," said Naan, "I guess that is a bit of a story."

"And what be your names again?" asked the youngling.

"Raef," said Raef, "I am Raef and this is my wife, Naan."

"Naan and Raef," Iris said to herself, "I completely forgot to get their names."

"You were never quiet long enough for us to tell you," mumbled Raef under his breath.

"Raef!" whispered Naan, as she slapped him.

"And where is Furry Hollow?" asked the girl. "It sounds kind of scary."

"*Fir*," said Raef, "Fir, like the trees. We live in *Fir* Hollow."

"There are furry trees?" asked Pari.

Raef laughed.

"Did it take you a whole season to get here?" Pari asked.

"I should tell the neighbors," said Iris, before Naan or Raef could answer.

"Those are funny shoes," said Pari, looking at Naan's feet.

"Perhaps I should call a gathering," said Iris.

Raef looked at Naan, raising his eyebrows and grinning. He leaned closer to his wife and whispered, "We may have to wait until later to get some answers."

Iris spooned pottage into bowls carved from rock. Raef and Naan sat at a tiny table near the fire to eat. It was hard to imagine how Iris, her husband and Pari all fit at the table. Raef pulled his spoon from his belt as Iris put a tiny square saltcellar on the table. It too was carved from rock. The bowls and cellar, he noted, were covered in intricate carvings.

"Where do you get these bowls?" asked Raef.

"Oh, Tren makes them for us. He is quite the artisan."

"Artisan?" asked Naan, "I am an artisan as well, though I do not work in stone."

The pottage was better than Raef expected from such a small settlement. It tasted a bit wild, but he supposed that was to be expected this far from civilization. He pulled his knife from its scabbard and dipped the tip in salt to add to his pottage.

"I've never seen bowls used for pottage," said Raef, "I grew up eating off of trenchers."

Pari tilted her head and scratched it.

"That means old, dry bread," said Naan, "We eat our pottage off hard bread."

Pari wrinkled her nose, "Why would you eat off old bread?"

"Well…" Raef began, not entire certain how to answer, "to…to not waste anything, or leave dishes to wash."

He was pleased with his answer, though he had no idea if it was why the villages ate off trenchers.

"I think I will stay here in Promise, then," said Pari.

After they had eaten, Iris cleared the table and pulled up a stool at one end. Pari skipped around the table as they talked. Only, it was mostly Pari who did the talking, mostly questions, without waiting to hear the answers.

"Do you have any more younglings?"

"Are there lots of horses like yours in your village?"

"Is everyone tall like Raef?"

"Why is Raef's hair so long?"

"Are you a hunter or a gardener?"

"Do all the women in Fir Hollow have dresses with pretty flowers sewn on them like Naan's"

"Can you run really fast with those long legs?"

Raef and Naan had no opportunity to answer between questions.

A stocky man entered the hut and Iris and Pari fell silent. The man looked at Raef, then Naan, then little Nine. He looked confused or concerned, Raef could not tell which. Then he looked at Raef, appeared to study his face, and finally smiled.

"I'll bet your ears are ringing from these two," he said calmly, gesturing to his wife and daughter.

"Father, they are visitors from Furry Hollow," said Pari, "and they eat off moldy bread!"

The man squatted low and patted Pari on the head. Raef stood, out of respect, and the man stood and took his hand with a surprisingly firm grip.

"I am Siro, and this is my family, who you have obviously met."

"Daddy, Daddy," said Pari.

"You need to go wash up," the man said to Pari.

The youngling scampered off to a corner basin of water.

"I am Raef and this is my wife Naan."

Naan stood and bowed.

"And you have a little one, I see," said Siro.

"Yes, her name is 'Nine,'" said Naan.

"Nine!" said Siro, "well, that is unusual. At least for us. You are dusty, you should both wash up. I will show you where you can wash properly."

Siro led them outside. The hut was one in a circle of eight. At the center a large fire pit was smoldering, encircled with seats made of logs and stumps. The huts themselves were simpler than Raef had seen— made of poles and grass and a little mud. There were no thick timber frames or whitewashed walls. Beyond the far end of the circle of huts Raef saw a cultivated field with a few Laborers bent over and working. Surrounding the garden plot were three structures, two of them fairly large. One looked to be a stable.

Siro lead them to a well, not far from the fire pit. A large bucket hung over a round circle of stones. Raef could smell water below.

"You can wash up here at our communal well," said Siro. Then he bowed and left.

Raef and Naan did their best to clean the road dirt off their arms and faces. Nine protested loudly at the cold water as she was washed. Raef noted a few heads poke out of windows to look at them. A young man approached from the hut nearest Silo's and another woman descended on them from a hut across the circle. Several younglings scampered from huts and other hidden places to join the gathering.

"Well, here comes everyone," said Raef to Naan.

"Raef, be nice. These seem like wonderful people."

Siro re-emerged from his hut with Iris and Pari in tow. A circle formed at the well, the dirty-faced younglings hanging on the dresses of the women. The young man walked to Siro's side. Siro put his arm around the young man and looked at Raef.

"Raef and Naan, this is Tren, our only bachelor," said Siro.

The young man, who looked to have fewer seasons than Raef, blushed and nodded.

"And this is Wynn."

The woman who bowed to Raef and Naan had more seasons than the rest, but not that of an elderly woman. Some of the younglings clinging to her dress were as small or smaller than Pari.

"Come," said Siro, "the sun is growing strong. Sit by the fire pit with us."

Tren and Wynn followed Siro and Iris, along with Raef and Naan, to the pit. The younglings danced and played around them as they sat.

"Tell us," said Siro, "what brings your family to this isolated settlement?"

"We were not looking for a settlement," said Raef, "we were looking for a path to the mountains."

"You brought few provisions," interrupted Iris, "and you have a new baby."

Raef turned to look at Iris, surprised at her impertinence in the presence of three men.

"You cannot be explorers or scouts," said Siro.

"No, nothing like that," said Raef. He paused, trying to gather his courage, "We, um, we were seeking a man. A man said to live in one of these mountains."

Siro cocked his head to one side. Wynn grinned and glanced at Tren.

"We seek one called the Soul Healer," said Naan.

"Ah," said Siro, his eyes brightening, "that explains everything. Which of you is the Dragon

Child?"

Raef felt the blood drain from his face, "How… how did you know?"

"Who else would need a Soul Healer?" asked Wynn.

Raef jerked his head in Wynn's direction. *Are all the women in this place so rude?* He wondered.

Siro looked at Raef and chuckled.

"Young Intercessor," said Siro, "please excuse our lack of dignity. We do not follow the customs of the villages. We are a small settlement, and women are given the same standing as men. We can ill afford asking our women to keep silent in men's company when we need all the voices of wisdom we can get."

Raef tried to compose himself. Naan leaned toward Siro, apparently quite willing to accept this arrangement.

"Then, you know of this man?" asked Naan.

"The Soul Healer?" asked Siro, "yes we know him well. He lives near the top of the mountain. His name is Tup."

"And this, this Tup," said Raef, "He knows how to help people who…who are under…"

"Under Rail's spell?" asked Siro.

Raef sat back, alarmed to hear the dragon's name spoken in public. It was forbidden to speak the name of the great beast out loud.

Siro smiled and placed his hand on Raef's leg.

"There is no reason to fear," said Siro, "the dragon does not come here. It is not welcome. We are not afraid to speak its name. We have come to understand that speaking Rail's name reduces its power over us."

Raef shook his head, trying to understand. His wife seemed unaffected by the shocking disregard for proper practice.

"Can you show us to this Tup?" asked Naan.

"It is a fair journey," said Siro, "we will need to make preparations. But yes, one of us will take you. Tonight you will sleep here."

"We thank you for your generosity," Raef managed to say.

"It is nothing," said Iris, "each of us here was once a newcomer, with no place to stay."

"We can stay in our cart," said Raef, "we have a tent for a covering."

"You will do no such thing, young Intercessor," said Wynn, "we will find room for you. Summer is still new and you will find it gets quite cold here at sunset."

"We…we have also run out of provisions," said Naan.

"We should have enough to share with you," said Tren, "do you not think so, Siro?"

"Yes, we will make do," Siro replied, "Come, Raef, we can get your belongings while Naan and your baby rest."

Siro and Tren stood and walked behind the huts to collect the cart. Raef hurried to follow. The horse was put in a stall in the stable, which also housed sheep and other animals.

After last meal the settlement made a fire in the central pit and sat to visit. There were too many new faces and names for Raef to remember. Seven couples and Tren made up the adults, and several younglings and greenlings, which scurried about, making them too difficult to count.

"What brings you to us?" asked a man called Ian, who appeared to be the eldest.

"They seek Tup," said Siro.

"Ah," said Ian, "and are you the Dragon Child, then?"

Raef felt himself blush. *Why do these people keep calling out my shame?* He wondered.

"Yes," said Siro, "you never did say which of you was branded by Rail."

"I...it was...it was me," Raef stammered.

"You mean, it *is* you," said Ian with a grin, "It is not so hard to see it in you."

Raef looked at the man, who was nearly as old as his father. There was kindness in his eyes, but his gaze made Raef tremble.

"You were right to come," said Ian, "and fortunate to find us. This collective is known to very few."

"I am certain he had help finding us," said Siro, slapping Raef's shoulder. Raef looked at him, confused.

Siro stood and walked to another group of people. Raef was glad when Naan came to sit by him, taking Siro's place. Ian turned to speak with a woman who appeared to be his wife. Raef did not like all these people knowing why he was here. He remained silent, avoiding conversation until the circle broke up and people returned to their huts.

Tren took them into his hut for the night. They

made a temporary bed of straw from the stable but had to do without a privacy curtain, as Tren did not have one. It was quite cold that night, Raef discovered. He hoped they would not need to stay in this settlement long.

4

The inhabitants of Promise were already at work when Raef and Naan emerged from Tren's hut after first meal. Four men sat around the dead fire pit, apparently preparing for a hunt, inspecting spears, bows and arrows. Three women and Tren walked to the cultivated patch of land. Still others were milling around the stable and barn.

Raef looked to the sun, seeing it was still new in the sky. Ian and Siro approached Raef, each carrying a cloth-wrapped bundle.

"Did I miss homage?" asked Raef.

"Homage?" asked Ian.

Raef gazed around the small settlement, searching for a structure that might serve as a Ceremonial Lodge. He did not see one.

"Homage, you know, when the Keepers bless the villagers before work," said Raef.

"Ah," said Siro, "I have heard of those ceremonies. We have no Intercessor clan here."

"You do not follow the ceremonies?"

"We have a small celebration for the changing of

seasons," said Ian, "but most of us left the villages when we were yet younglings. We do not recall such things."

Raef straightened his back and studied the two men before him. *Only the slovenly and degenerate would fail to observe homage in Fir Hollow,* he thought. *Then again,* he realized, *villagers in Fir Hollow ignored the dangers of the dragon, which is, perhaps no better.*

Naan stepped to his side, smiled and gazed downward.

"Thank you again for taking us in," she said, "we are not even of your kin."

"Of course," said Ian, "Come, we have something for you."

Raef followed the men, his wife and daughter in tow. Near the fire pit Siro paused and lifted two shoulder bags from the ground.

"These are for you and Naan," said Ian, "provisions for your journey."

Raef took the bundles and slung both over his shoulder.

"Thank you," said Naan, "that is very kind."

"I will show you the trail head," said Siro, "it is a full sun's journey to where Tup lives. He will have you stay with him at least one sun, then you will return here."

Raef and Naan followed as Siro as he led them past the circle of huts, through a large grassy area, and to the base of the mountain. A small footpath led upward.

"You will not be lost as long as you keep to the path," said Siro.

Raef bowed slightly and turned toward the path. He took a deep breath, trying to calm his nerves, then stepped to the path. Trees closed around them as they began to climb the slope before them.

"Raef, you did not even give Siro a parting word."

"I did not realize. I am sorry my mind is distracted. I am apprehensive about meeting this... this Soul Healer."

Raef plodded alongside his wife, the sun seeming to climb more slowly than normal. The air was damp and cool against his face. Drips echoed through the trees, though Raef could not see the source of the sound. He began to pant, not accustomed to such steep terrain. He looked down at his wife, who smiled up at him, though her face gleamed with perspiration. Nine cooed up at him. He put his eyes back to the trail and trudged on.

As the sun rose, the path began to twist and turn with sharp switchbacks. Raef's foot slipped on a damp, flat rock. He assisted Naan past it so she would not fall. His lungs heaved, gasping in the high elevation. He heard his wife panting behind him.

By mid sun Raef's legs began to ache. They paused to eat a hurried meal, and then Raef took Nine so Naan could rest her arms as they continued up the mountain.

Nine seemed quite happy with the trip. Her eyes were wide as they passed sights she had never seen. The only noises she made were gentle coos. They stopped to feed her twice. She did not nap after mid sun, as was her usual habit. Her eyes remained wide and mouth agape.

The air-cooled further after mid sun and became filled with the musty scent of moss. Mud squished with each of Raef's steps, soiling his shoes nearly up to the laces. He glanced down, dismayed at his ruined deerskin shoes. *They are new,* he dismayed, *purchased only a moon-cycle past.*

They stopped to rest at a flat area next to the trail as the sun approached the horizon and the light grew dim.

"It appears we are near the top," said Raef, "but I do not see any sign of this Healer."

"Siro would not have sent us if he were not here," said Naan.

After a short rest they continued up the trail. Soon Raef caught a glimpse of a faint, gray wisp floating up between the trees.

"Look, there," said Raef, "someone has made a fire."

Beyond the trees he could just make out the outline of a structure. As they approached, he could see it was constructed of logs, and tightly surrounded by trees. It looked as if another hut, a bit smaller, was beyond it. The smoke came from the first building.

"I suppose we have arrived," said Raef, his stomach becoming tight with apprehension.

He felt Naan touch his arm. He looked down to see her smiling.

"I know he will help us," she said.

"I wish I was as certain."

They approached the shack, stopping a few paces before the door.

"Tup!" called Raef, "is there one here called

'Tup?'"

The door creaked open and a snowy-haired head peeked out. He was a diminutive, bearded fellow.

"Are you Tup?" Raef asked.

The man swung the door open and stepped out, turning his gaze from Raef to Naan and smiling. He wore a robe, but not that of an Intercessor. It was a hooded robe of emerald wool, glinting with strands of glowworm silk. The man wore silver rabbit fur boots and held a knurled staff as tall as he. Raef felt a chill run up his spine as he gazed at the staff. A soft blue glow shined magically through the many cracks that ran up the shaft.

"A wizard!" said Raef, taking three steps back.

The small man walked to face Naan. They seemed to lock eyes, remaining uncomfortably silent.

"You look sad," said the wizard to Naan, "but you can rest now. You no longer need carry this alone."

Tears began to stream down Naan's cheeks, which surprised Raef. The wizard reached out and stroked her hair and put his palm on little Nine's head.

"Get away from my wife!" called Raef.

Naan and the wizard ignored him.

"And who is this?"

"This is our baby, Nine."

"Nine. My, what a wonderful calling."

Nine cooed at the stranger, grinning broadly. He beamed back, and then very slowly turned his gaze Raef. The wizard had to tilt his head up to meet Raef's eyes.

"And you are the Dragon Child."

Raef furrowed his brow. The man extended his hand to Raef's chest. Raef froze, too shocked to move, as the wizard untied the top three cords of Raef's tunic. The small man placed his hand against Raef's upper chest. The wizard's hand stung Raef's skin and Raef backed away. He rubbed his chest, his skin still hot from the wizard's touch.

"I will have nothing to do with you, wizard," Raef said.

"Oh," said the wizard, his eyebrows lifting, "and why is this, young Intercessor?"

Raef took another step back. It did not comfort him that a wizard recognized he was an Intercessor.

"You wield the power of unclean spirits," said Raef.

"Oh, do I?"

Raef raised his voice, "You defile the ways of Zul!"

The small man grinned slowly, "Are you certain it is *I* who has defiled the Great Spirit?"

Raef straightened, stepping closer to the wizard.

"I am not any Intercessor, you worker of evil," said Raef, "I am the son of a Keeper, and a Keeper myself, chosen by Zul."

The man inspected his palm, his smile fading, and then looked back to Raef.

"Then Zul has not chosen wisely," said the wizard, "for you have been with Rail a very long time. And to Black Rock as well, have you not?"

Raef's blood ran cold. The wizard's smile returned.

"I am Tup," said the wizard, "I am a Soul Healer."

"He does not like that wizard, does he," said Zul.

"You are being a bit cruel, do you not think?" asked Erif.

The image of Raef and Naan faded with a ripple. Erif looked up and squinted into the sun. He could see there would be no rain…again.

"He has to let go of what he believes," said the old spirit, "you know that."

"I do know, but it can feel cruel, having something thrown in ones face like that."

Zul did not respond, continuing to gaze into the empty pool.

"Am I to train today?" asked the Warrior.

"No. Record what you have seen in the scroll. Do whatever you like after that."

Erif stood and Zul faced him. "Zul, I must be ready when I face Rail."

"The scrolls are more important," said the ancient spirit, "Others can fight Rail if need be, but only you can write the scrolls."

Erif scratched his head, "Could you not show these visions to someone else?"

"It would not be the same," said Zul. The spirit faded from sight.

Erif sighed, and then walked back to camp. He removed a half-finished scroll from a wooden box, unrolled it, and began to write.

PART TWO

SOUL HEALER

5

Raef ducked his head down to enter the small hut but still smaked his head on the doorframe. He rubbed his head and squinted against the pain. He stuffed the urge to curse as he searched for a place to sit in the tiny hut.

Tup's shack was nicer than Raef expected from the outside. The center fire pit was lined with round river rock, four stones tall. The dirt floor was covered in small rugs, an unusual feature, but one Raef imagined made sense up here on the frigid mountain. Naan and Tup were already seated around a round table made of a dark wood Raef was not familiar with. He took a seat on the remaining empty stool and waited expectantly. Nine began to squirm in Naan's arms. Raef took the baby from Naan, held her to his chest, and patted her back.

"I need to know how long you have been visiting Rail," said Tup.

"Since I was a youngling," said Raef, "I think I had only six seasons."

Tup's expression grew more serious.

"How often did you visit it, when you lived in your village?"

"It is hard to recall. I suppose nearly every sun by the time I reached ten seasons."

"And when did it take you to Black Rock?"

How does he know so much about Rail? Raef wondered.

"When I had thirteen seasons. I had just become a greenling. The dragon flew into my village and took me, right in front of everyone."

"But you returned to your village later?" asked Tup.

Raef tried to remember how it had all happened, tilting his head in thought.

"I tried to go back home, when I had fifteen seasons," Raef began, "I made it all the way back to Fir Hollow. But I could not make myself enter. I was afraid of what they would say to me. Then Rail came to get me and I went back to Black Rock with it."

Raef paused, eyeing the wizard's reaction. The old man had a gentle smile and showed no alarm, so Raef continued.

"Three seasons later, when I was no longer a greenling, I returned to Fir Hollow again. That time I was not…I was going to say I was not afraid. I was afraid, of what they would think of me. They had seen the dragon take me. They knew where I had been. But I could not stay at Black Rock anymore. I just could not."

Tup sat back and looked at the ceiling, rubbing his stubby beard.

"Very few return from Black Rock," Tup said.

"Black Rock will make this more difficult for you, but the fact you escaped on your own is a good sign."

Naan looked at Raef and smiled weakly.

"I did not really escape," said Raef, "Rail just let me leave."

"Raef," said Tup, "everyone at Black Rock can leave. Rail can stop no one. The problem is that very few have the courage to leave. Just a few, like yourself."

"I am not courageous," said Raef, looking to the ground.

"If you left Black Rock you are," said Tup.

Raef felt a flutter within. Perhaps he could dare to hope. Just a little.

"Rail's power is not in its size," said Tup, "The dragon's power is in deception. That, and its essence."

"Its what?" asked Rail.

"Its essence," repeated Tup, "Raef, before it took you to Black Rock, did the dragon ever lick you?"

Raef recoiled at the question and looked away. He did not like remembering such things. He felt his face burn hot. He did not want to answer. It was embarrassing.

"Would you rather Naan leave for a moment?" asked Tup.

"No, no," said Raef, "She can hear." He took a deep breath, "Yes. Rail was always trying to lick my head, when I was very small even."

"Just your head?" asked Tup.

Raef squirmed, remembering the sickly sweat odor of dragon drool, cringing at how it felt on his skin.

"Why do you have to know?" asked Raef.

Tup did not respond.

"It…it seemed to want to lick down the back of my neck," said Raef, "but I hated it when it did that."

"Ah, and that went on for many seasons, did it not?"

"I…I suppose."

"Raef, if the dragon had not soaked you in its essence for all those seasons, you would have left Black Rock as soon as you could," said Tup. "Even if you had enjoyed playing with the dragon back in your village, the sight of Black Rock and the Dragon Children would have been too revolting for you to consider staying."

Raef recalled the first sight of grown men and women covered in filth, their clothing hanging off them in shreds. The terrible, foul odor that was everywhere.

"I never understood why I did not run away," said Raef, "I could see how revolting it was, but I stayed anyway."

"Rail's saliva is not like that of other beasts," explained Tup, "It is full of the dragon's essence. The fluid soaks through the skin and intoxicates the victims, putting them in a sort of trance."

"Rail was poisoning me?"

"In a manner of speaking."

"What does this essence do," asked Naan, "what did it do to Raef?"

"A number of things," said Tup, "but the effect increases the more essence you are subjected Let me show you."

Tup shifted and looked at Raef, "Raef, what did Rail look like the first time you saw it?"

"Ugly," said Raef quickly, "it was hideous. It was all oily looking and its face was gruesome."

"Then why did you continue to return to it?"

Raef hung his head, "Because…because I am flawed. I liked it, in spite of its vileness."

"You are not flawed, Raef," said Tup, "and you did not return to it alone, did you?"

Surprise ran through Raef's veins. He raised his head to look at Tup.

"How do you know all this?" asked Raef, "Yes, an older friend took me to see it. I remember I could not understand why he did not notice how hideous the dragon was."

"But eventually the dragon no longer appeared repulsive," said Tup, "in fact, it became quite beautiful."

"Yes!" said Raef, flooded with gratitude that someone finally understood, "its appearance became different. But, how do you know this?"

The old man grinned, "I am a wizard, remember? Am I not supposed to posses dark powers?"

Raef sat back, smirking, "I suppose I deserved that."

"Raef, I have no evil sources, I assure you," said Tup. "The dragon is predictable. Nothing you experienced is new. Your story is as old as the sun."

Raef relaxed a bit in his seat.

"So, tell me, Raef, how did the dragon appear to you, in the end?"

"It was…majestic," said Raef.

"Only to your eyes, Raef," said Tup, "and only because you were under the influence of its essence. The essence fogged your vision."

"But sometimes," said Raef, "even at Black Rock, the dragon was ugly again. It was as if there were times it looked like when I first saw it, ugly and gruesome."

"Interesting," said Tup, rubbing his chin, "that too is a good sign."

"Does the essence wear off," asked Naan, "after many suns or seasons?"

"No," said Tup, "it remains inside you, a part of you. And as more is given to you, the effect grows stronger."

"Black Rock," said Raef, "it made us all…it licked everyone, a lot."

"Yes," said Tup, "it has complete access to its victims at Black Rock. There it demands its essence be received, in great quantities."

Raef saw Naan squirm. He did not want her to know how he remained shirtless all those season in the Great Basin as Rail walked among the Dragon Children, dropping its serpent-like tongue on them and wetting their backs. He cringed, recalling the slime.

"Such evil," said Naan.

Raef sat stunned. So much made sense now. And they had only just met the Soul Healer named Tup.

The wizard leaned forward and took one of Naan's hands and one of Raef's. His expression grew serious.

"I must be fair to both of you," the little man

began, "yes, it is possible for Raef to become free from Rail's influence, but it is neither a short nor easy process. Most do not have the patience for what is required in soul healing. And for one who has been to Black Rock, it is all that much more difficult. The essence is strong in Raef, and purging is unpleasant. He will want to quit. He will, at times, want to return to Black Rock. His chances are, I must confess, slim."

Raef felt as if he might cry. He had to look away.

"But, have you not helped others who have been to Black Rock?" Naan asked.

"Yes, a few," said Tup, "and as I said, Raef's escape shows courage, but anyone who has been to Black Rock, especially for as long as five seasons, has been deeply influenced by Rail."

Naan looked at Raef, smiling weakly. Tup turned his gaze to Raef.

"It took many seasons for this much essence to be put in you. It will take many seasons to rid your body of it as well. And being so young when it began, you mind will have been bent and twisted. That will require retraining."

Raef felt his stomach sink at the man's words, "Many seasons?"

"Yes, no less than five seasons."

"I have to stay here for five seasons?" Raef nearly shouted.

Without answering, Tup turned to face Naan.

"And I must be fair to you, young woman. Very few marriages are able to survive after one partner has been to Black Rock. The odds are against you both. There is hope, and it has been done before, but it would be dishonest with you to say the chances of your marriage surviving are good."

Naan sat back in her chair as her lips began to tremble.

"Naan," Tup continued, "any chance for your marriage to survive will require you learn the secrets of Rail. As Raef begins to change you will need to know which changes are for good and which are for evil."

"But, this is not my fault!" said Naan, "I did nothing wrong!"

"No," said Tup quietly, "none of this is your fault. But if you wish to stay with Raef you have no choice. It would be too dangerous for you and Nine otherwise. Rail will attack your family when Raef tries to break free of it. The dragon believes Raef belongs to it. Rail will not let go easily."

Naan put her head in her hands and cried. Tup held Naan's arm, wishing he could ease her sorrow.

"The next step is yours to take, Raef," said Tup, "how badly do you wish to be free of Rail's influence? Enough to spend five seasons in Promise? Enough to come up to this mountain to see me each moon cycle?"

Raef found he could not answer.

"And Naan," Tup continued, "do you want to stay with Raef so badly that you are willing to stay here with him?"

Naan began to cry again.

"Do not answer now," said Tup.

Raef watched Naan's countenance. She looked crushed. He felt afraid.

I do not think I can go through this without Naan, he realized, *But she does not look strong enough to face this.*

"Who has done this before?" asked Raef, "who has been to Black Rock, escaped, and become free of Rail's essence?"

"They were rescued from Black Rock, they did not escape," said Tup, "They live below, in Promise. You have met them."

"All of them?" Naan asked.

"No," said Tup, "but half the adults in Promise once lived in Black Rock."

"And you," asked Naan, "where you once a...a Dragon Child?"

"No," said Tup, "I apprenticed as a Soul Healer under an old Keeper, ages past."

"A Keeper?" asked Raef. "A Keeper trained a wizard? I have never heard such a thing. Besides, Keepers know nothing of Rail, they are completely ignorant of it."

"Some know more than you realize," said Tup. "But you are correct, Keepers in this age are usually blind to what Rail's true threat is. But in the past, in the previous era, it was the duty of the Keepers to protect the villagers' minds from Rail. And, to heal the souls of those who fell prey to its seduction."

Raef shook his head. It was difficult to believe Keepers ever spoke openly of Rail, much less had the power to heal its victims.

"Sadly," Tup continued, "the Keepers have since lost their vision and are indifferent or ignorant. The dragon has free reign over the villages now. I fear its influence is growing so strong it may ensnare the entire Province. It is a dark age."

Tup waved his hand through the air, "Enough for now. It is time for last meal. Stay as many suns as you need, but make your decisions before you return to Promise. Once each of you has decided what you will do, I will tell you how we will proceed. That is, of course, if you choose healing. If not, you can be on your way."

Naan looked away and did not speak to Raef. Raef wanted to ask her what she was thinking, but he feared how Naan would answer.

6

"It appears that Naan and I will be staying in Promise
for…a number of seasons," said Raef.

Ian, the man standing before him was the elder
of Promise.

"You will need a hut for your family," said the
man, "We will help you build it next sunrise. For now
you can sleep in Tren's hut once more. He has the
most room, being a bachelor."

Raef took a ragged breath. *It is done*, he thought,
I'm staying here…for who knows how long.

The following sunrise Raef found that most of
the village had assembled around the fire pit. He
joined them to discover they were discussing building
a hut for Raef and Naan. The plans were completed
and some were sent to cut poles, others grass, and a
few to collect mud in wooden barrels. Ura, who was
Ian's wife, along with a few other women, collected
Naan and baby Nine, taking them away somewhere
with no explanation to Raef. Ian motioned Raef to
follow him to the spot where the new hut was to be
built.

They stopped at the opposite side of the circle from Tren's hut, near one corner of the cultivated field.

Raef looked around him as men scurried about. He had never built anything before, the closest being supervising the repair of several thatched roofs back in his home village, but even then he had mostly watched.

Poles clattered to the ground as greenling and young men returned with supplies. Raef started to bend down to pick one up.

"Wait, my impatient friend," said Ian, "post holes must be dug first."

Raef stepped back as more supplies were brought. A pair of men returned from a small structure near the field, carrying digging tools.

Raef tried to help as his hut was assembled, but he found he was in the way more than he was any help. He cracked a pole by pounding it into the ground too hard. He tied joints together, only for them to come undone shortly after. He used too much mud making the sod walls and the straw fell to the ground rather than stay in place. As the sun approached mid-sky Raef stood back and looked down at himself. He was covered in filth, far more than anyone else, yet he was unsure if he had helped at all. He pushed down a sudden urge to run into the woods and leave Promise behind.

One of the men stopped, stretched his back and looked up at the sun.

"Ian, I believe it is time to go," said the man.

Ian glanced up at the sun, "I see that it is."

Men began to gather around Ian. Tren, who had been working in the garden, came to join them as well. Raef counted seven men, which he believed was all but one of the men in Promise. Ian turned and began to walk out past the cultivated field. The other men followed, so Raef joined them.

"Where are we going?" asked Raef, following them.

"The sun is high," said a man next to Ian, "Which is best for purging."

"Purging?" asked Raef.

"Getting the essence out of us," said a young man.

Raef was embraced to hear the subject mentioned out loud, "Why...why do you need purging?" he asked Ian, quietly.

Ian smiled at Raef, his eyes crinkling at the sides as he did.

"It has been many seasons since we had a novice among us," said the older man, "Young Raef, I must undergo purging because, like you, I am a Dragon Child."

Raef looked around, wide-eyed, to see who might have heard. Ian laughed rather loudly.

"What is it, old man?" someone asked Ian.

"Raef is concerned that you heard me admit that I was a Dragon Child."

The new man laughed, clasping a hand to Raef's shoulder. "Raef, we are all Dragon Children. I am called Evot."

"And I am Kaz," said a man who appeared to have around thirty seasons.

"I am Ramey," said another, who looked to have no more seasons than Raef, "And you already know Tren."

"Everyone in Promise is a Dragon Child?" asked Raef.

"Not everyone," said Ramey, "But all of us here are."

"And some of the women," said Tren.

"*Were* Dragon Children," interrupted Ian, "we no longer go by that calling."

Raef followed the men beyond the stable to a vast grassy area. In the center of the meadow was a short mound on which grew no grass. The seven men stepped up onto the hill, forming a circle, which Raef joined. Then the men began removing their tunics. The hairs on the back of Raef's neck stood up. While all men went bare-chested in Black Rock, it was unheard of for a man to disrobe in public in civilized society.

"Come, Raef," said Ian, "remove your tunic."

Raef stood, slack-jawed at the sight of seven shirtless men lowering their heads to the center, exposing their backs to the sun. Then Raef saw the scars.

The back of each man was covered with scars, some round, and some oval in shape. Not scars, as one would acquire by injury, but like the aftermath of festering sores that had healed poorly.

"Your shirt?" said Siro.

Raef slowly untied the front laces of his tunic to loosen it and lifted it over his head. He wore an undergarment that he removed as well, standing half-naked in front of seven men he scarcely knew. He wanted to ask about the scars, but decided against it. Raef hung his head, like the others.

"Bare your back to the sun," said Ian.

Raef pulled his long hair off his back, and draped it over one shoulder, exposing his back and neck to the sun. Glancing side to side, Raef noticed some men's backs were riddled with scars, scarcely a spot unblemished, while others had only scattered pocks across their backs.

Then the burning began, as if someone were dripping drops of boiling water in spots across his back.

"Ah!" said Raef, "what is that?"

"Your skin burning?" asked Evot.

"Yes!"

"The essence comes to the surface in direct sunlight," said Ian, "It can be a bit painful at first."

"A bit?" said Raef, flinching.

Raef clenched his eyelids, feeling his skin stretching painfully in three spots on his back. One burst and he felt an oily liquid dripping down his skin. He felt a small flame burning his skin, and then vanish. He grimaced, determined not to cry out in pain again.

"My back...is leaking."

Tren glanced around Raef's back.

"I am afraid it is," said the young man.

"And something caught fire!" said Raef.

"Strong sunlight ignites the essence, when it reaches the air," said Ian.

"Am...am I going to look like all of you?" asked

Raef.

"You mean the scars on our backs," said Siro, "yes, Raef, that has to happen. It is the only way to remove the essence."

Raef felt his countenance sag. He did not want to be disfigured. He did not want to be forever marked.

The weeping continued from his three ruptured boils, slowly dripping down his skin. His skin sizzled. He could hear it. It was too late. He would look like them. As if it was not enough to lose his status as Keeper and leave the Intercessor class in disgrace, now he would live his life as a physically blemished man.

Raef steeled his face, realizing he was near tears, and directed his attention to the men around him. He noticed their backs were not weeping, not like his. A few had a slight dampness around the old scars on their backs, but that might also be sweat. He was afraid to ask about it. He wished he could put his tunic on. Or undergo the purging alone. It was humiliating to be seen like this. He felt a fourth blister raise painfully on his back and burst.

After an unbearably long time under the sun, Ian finally said it was time to get back to work. Raef's back stung when his shirt touched his back and he felt bloody spots sticking to the fabric. Raef walked at the back of the group as they returned to the huts, Siro by his side.

"Siro," Raef said, "there is something I do not understand."

"What is that?"

Raef winced as his shirt pulled away from one of the bloodied spots on his back. "This did not happen when I was at Black Rock. I walked the Great Basin five seasons with no tunic on my back."

Siro grinned up at Raef, then put his hand on his shoulder. "Do you not remember how few stars were visible after sunset? Do you not remember how faint the sun after it rose?"

Raef pondered the question. It was true, he saw but a fraction of the stars in the Great Basin he had seen from Fir Hollow. It was also true that after sunrise the sky had always been mostly gray.

"Yes," said Raef, "yes, I do remember that."

"The full sun does not reach the basin," said Siro, "it cannot penetrate the mist."

"Mist?"

"The mist that hangs eternally over the basin. The sun cannot get through, at least not enough to heat the essence."

"Is that why the dragon takes its children there?"

"Rail hides its children in the caldera. I imagine the mist is its own doing. It is a powerful spirit, we must remember."

They reached the circle of huts and Raef went to his cart. Naan was waiting in their cart with mid sun meal prepared.

"What happened to your back?" asked Naan, who turned Raef around so he faced away from her. "There are blood spots on your tunic."

"Ow!" he said, as he felt his shirt pull away from one of his wounds, tearing the new scab off.

He turned to face Naan. Her eyes were wide.

"They made me remove my tunic and undershirt," he told her, "The sun made my back blister and the essence came out. The essence ignites when it reaches the sun."

Naan winced, "I am so sorry, Raef. That sounds terrible."

Naan was quiet, looking at the ground.

"I had to bathe in a log," said Naan, "soaking in water mixed with some kind of oil."

"Bathe in a log?"

"Enormous cedar logs, cut in half and hollowed out. Some other women bathed as well. They were all wives of Dragon Children."

"What in all the Province for?"

"They put oils in the water that remove any essence from my skin."

"Why would you have essence?"

"From you, Raef. The essence can rub off on another person."

Raef stared at the ground, unable to speak. It was not fair for his wife to have to endure anything unpleasant because of him.

Naan handed him a bowl of half-cold porridge.

"This is from Ura," said Naan, "until we have a place to prepare our own food."

Raef ate next to his wife in silence. Nine cooed and giggled on his lap.

"Two of the women," Naan said, breaking the silence, "two of them have been to Black Rock. Those women did purging in the sun like you describe. But they do it away from the others, for privacy I think."

"Which women have been to Black Rock?" asked

Raef.

"Evot's wife, Garma, and a woman called Wynn."

"Who is Wynn's husband?"

"She said his calling is Bolin. He is not a Dragon Child," said Naan.

Raef finished eating and picked up Naan, who grasped his lip in her tiny hand.

"Was it bad?" asked Naan, "the purging."

"Painful enough to make a man cry out."

"I am sorry, husband," she said, gently touching a spot near one of his sores.

"I do not know if we can do this," he said.

"Raef, we have to. It is this, or you need to return to that dragon and leave Nine and I to fend for ourselves."

"I...I do not want that."

"Then let us try," she said, holding his face in her hands, "I will try if you will."

7

"That was a cabbage seedling," said the greenlia next to Raef.

Raef paused, hoe in mid swing, and looked at the plant he had just uprooted.

That was not a weed? He though to himself.

Raef glanced down the row he had been working on since sunup. Many similar looking plants lay stricken in the ditch. He let out a ragged sigh. The young female smiled at him.

"I am sorry," said Raef, "I have never been good at deciphering plants."

"It is not so hard," the greenlia said, "look how the color of the leaf is different. It has a blue hue to it, not like the weeds, which are very green."

Raef looked down at the severed cabbage. He could not see much difference in its color. He wondered how many crops he had destroyed since sunrise. He took a deep breath and determined to watch more carefully.

At mid sun Raef left the field with the other workers, all of who were female, save himself and the bachelor, Tren.

"How goes the farming?" shouted Evot, as Raef neared the circle of huts. Evot's tunic had a fresh smear of blood down its front. His hunt had obviously gone well.

"You likely will not want me out there much longer," said Raef, "I believe I have destroyed a fair amount of your crop."

"Nonsense," said Evot, "you will do fine."

Raef hung his head. He wished Evot would not try to cheer him up. It was true, Raef, knew, he had no talent for working with plants. Raef veered away from Evot as they walked. The man chased after, coming closer to Raef.

"If you like, you may join us in a hunt next sunrise," said Evot.

"I have no skill with the bow," said Raef, "I…I never trained as a youngling."

"Ah. Well, no matter, we need help in the field as well. Crops are provisions every bit as much as meat."

Raef smiled weakly, and then turned to his hut. Naan was already inside. She had a sad look on her face.

"How was it?" he asked.

"I miss my work in Fir Hollow," she said, "I was an artisan there. Here they have me carving spoons from tree limbs."

"That sounds more interesting than hoeing weeds."

"Yes, it does, I suppose."

Raef sat wearily on a stump at a tiny table that had been built for them. Naan put a small loaf of bread on the table and a bowl of cabbage pottage. He picked up the bowl and turned it in his hand. It was carved of gray rock but polished to shine like steel. Leaves had been carved around its upper rim on the outside.

"Where did this come from?" he asked.

"From Tren," said Naan, "He carves them, remember?"

"I have never seen anything like it. I have seen ceramic ceremonial bowls, but this must have taken over a moon-cycle to carve."

Naan held her bowl up and examined it, "I wonder where he finds the time to do such work. I have never seen the like of it either, and I am an artisan."

Raef spooned out some pottage. It was bland, but he did not comment to Naan. "Perhaps he carves in winter," he said, "what else would there be to do here?"

After mid sun meal Raef accompanied the seven men who had been Dragon Children behind the stables to stand shirtless in the sun. His back was becoming gnarled and full of blistered boils. The pain was still as great, if not more so, than when he first exposed himself to the sun's brightness.

"Your face is downcast today, Raef," said Ian.

"It is nothing," said Raef.

"It is never nothing," said a young man called Jesson.

"You would not understand," said Raef, "you are a Warrior."

"A Warrior?" said Jesson, "we have no Warriors

here in Promise."

"You are a hunter. In Fir Hollow, where I was born, it was the Warriors who did most of the hunting. They were the brave ones."

"How are you not brave?" asked Tren.

Raef did not want to answer. He was afraid it would offend Tren. After all, Raef had never seen Tren hunt either.

"Speak up," said Evot.

"I have become a common Laborer," said Raef.

"Laborer? We all labor here," said Ian, "we have to."

"No, I mean as in a member of the Labor class. The lowest cast of the village."

"We do not have casts here," said Evot, "we all do our part."

"Of course you have," said Raef, "Ian is the elder, just like the Noble class back home. Most of the men are hunters, like Warriors."

"And that makes you and the women Laborers?" asked Evot.

"Most of them are only greenlias!" said Raef, "Even the women do more than I."

There was silence. Raef grimaced as a new boil expanded and burst on his back. Fluid oozed out, dripping down only a finger's width before sizzling into vapor. He bit his lip so not to cry out.

"I heard you were a Keeper once," said Siro, "That probably felt really important."

Raef wanted to speak but did not. He wanted to say it would be nice to have something good to hope for after loosing so much. After loosing his honor, his relatives and friends.

"None of that matters here," Siro continued, "We just have to let the past go."

After the purging, Raef and Tren returned to the crop field. Tren joined Raef, standing in the adjacent row. Raef inspected each plant carefully before deciding if it needed to be removed or not. By three quarter sun, Tren had left Raef far behind. Raef paused and turned to see how far Tren was ahead of him when a young female voice interrupted him.

"Sir, Raef," said a young greenlia, "those are bean sprouts you are pulling up. See, their leaves are smaller than the weeds."

It was all Raef could do to keep from kicking the bean sprout out of the ground and shouting curses. It was only for the tender years of the greenlia that he did not.

Raef returned to his hut when the sun lowered near the trees. Naan served venison for last meal, a gift from Siro, along with more cabbage pottage. Raef did not speak to Naan during the meal, though she tried to start conversation with him. Raef held his bowl, sliding his fingers over Tren's intricate carvings as he ate.

Even Tren has talents more than I, he thought to himself.

"I am taking Nine to sit out by the fire," said Naan, after they had both eaten.

"I am tired," said Raef, "I think I will stay here and have some hot tea."

He watched Naan leave, then pulled his sitting stump up near a wall and sat with his back reclined against its coolness. When he closed his eyes, Promise melted away. The dragon was waiting for him in his mind; its wings arched high to block the sun. Raef felt himself smile. It wasn't real, but it was comforting.

The next sunrise Raef work with a start. He looked around but found or heard nothing that might have woken him. The fresh straw under him pricked gently at his legs. Naan was still sleeping. He stood and walked to the lone window, cracking open the shudder. Only the slightest sliver of light was visible over the treetops. His heart sank recalling his visions of Rail.

I've done it again, he thought, *even if it was only my imagination, I went back to the dragon.*

He walked to the fire and stoked it to life, then hung a small iron pot of water over it to heat for tea. Naan began to stir as he was putting bread on the table.

"Raef, thank you for starting first meal," said Naan, as she got up.

"Anything for you," he smiled, trying to hide the shame he felt.

"Are you working in the fields again?" asked Naan.

"That is what I have been told. For the indefinite future, or until I destroy the entire crop."

Naan laughed. Nine woke up. Raef sighed and hoped he did better in the field than the last sun.

"Must I really write all this down?" asked Erif.
"You must," said Zul.

Erif waited for an explanation, but seeing the spirit gaze out to sea he returned his attention to the scroll. He selected a small stone to put on the upper edge to prevent the wind from lifting the scroll as he wrote. He dipped his quill into the hollowed stone of ink, and then continued writing. The whinny of a horse broke Erif's concentration.

"Your stallion seems to need attention," said Zul.

"To think I broke that beast not so long ago," said Erif, not looking up from his work, "and now it begs to be ridden."

"And where is your little friend?" asked Zul, "the coyote you keep as a pet."

"You are the spirit," said Erif, "you tell me. I have not seen her in five suns. Were not you the one who sent her to me for company?"

"I am certain she will return soon," said Zul.

"Of course you are," said Erif. "All done!" Erif rolled up the scroll and tied it with a strand of grass.

"Protect the scrolls well," said Zul, "they are of the highest importance."

"No one will want to read these," said Erif. "No one will want to believe them."

"Not everyone, no. But the ones who need to will."

"Are you certain…" Erif began, but when he looked up the Great Spirit was gone.

8

"Thank you, Siro, but I really can make it on my own. It is only one sun's journey." Raef said.

"I am certain you could," said Siro, "but until you are stronger you should not venture into the forest alone."

Raef hurried up the path toward the wizard's shack, wishing Siro would leave him be. "What in all the Province for?" asked Raef, "I am an adult."

"You are a Dragon Child," said Siro, "and the essence is still strong in you. You are still easy prey for Rail."

"Rail!" quipped Raef, "I would never visit that beast again. Not in the flesh."

Siro chuckled, "We all thought the same. But the dragon is crafty and will be more determined than ever to get you back, now that you have come to Promise."

"I am not a youngling, I do not need your help."

"Leaving the ways of a Dragon Child behind cannot be done alone, Raef. We, in Promise, have learned how to break free of the dragon's curse. Have you?"

Raef did not speak.

"Can you say you never dream of it?" asked Siro.

Raef tensed. He had imagined returning to Black Rock only a few suns past. He ceased his protest as Siro followed him up the path.

Tup was waiting with last meal prepared when they arrived. Naan, little Nine and Ura were in the tiny hut as well, having finished their time with Tup. The seating for all of them was impossibly cramped in the little hut.

"How was your visit with Tup?" Raef whispered to Naan.

"Thought provoking," she whispered back.

Raef raised his eyebrows, hoping for more, but Naan appeared to be done sharing.

After last meal all but Tup went to the sleeping shack behind Tup's hut. Raef wished to speak privately with his wife, hoping to learn more about what Tup had spoken with her about, but there was no opportunity. It was already dark and the visitor's hut was overcrowded with four adults, a baby and no privacy curtains. The men slept on the dirt floor while the women slept on the straw bedding.

The women parted the next sunrise. Tup served mugs of hot tea to Siro and Raef then asked Raef to follow him outside while Siro remained in the hut.

"Siro is not coming?" asked Raef.

"It is best that we talk alone, do you not think?" said Tup.

Raef found the arrangement awkward, perhaps even a little rude to Siro.

"Where are we going?" asked Raef.

"To the top!"

"The top of what?"

Tup did not answer but sauntered up the path, beyond the huts, sipping tea as he went. The trees thinned and became shorter as Raef followed. He panted in the thin air. Raef did not think he had ever been so high, other than perhaps with Rail when he rode it in the air. The trees became scarce, then absent entirely, with only long grass and shrubs on either side of the trail. Shortly they came to a flat, rocky place. They had arrived at the top of the mountain.

It was a drab, barren place, flat save for the odd boulder. Raef walked to the center and slowly turned. He could see to the ends of the Province in every direction. He could see the sea, far off to the south. The two larger of the Three Sisters Mountains obstructed his view to the west. North he could make out small tan pocks in the blanket of green. He squinted, and then realized the tan circles were Fir Hollow and other nearby villages. To the east was a vast emerald forest that extended beyond the villages, all the way to the looming darkness that was Black Rock. The home of Rail itself.

Raef ambled to the eastern edge, gazing blankly at the jagged outline of the mountain. What lay beyond the rim of Black Rock was obscured from view. But Raef had seen beyond what was visible. He had walked along the floor of the hidden caldera, circled by its rocky rim. He was no stranger to the Great Basin where all Dragon Children lived. He wondered how many were walking, blank-faced, in the mist-shrouded Basin as he stood watching.

Raef noticed Tup standing at his side and instantly averted his gaze, embarrassed to be caught staring at Black Rock. He found himself looking down a sheer rock cliff.

"That is quite a way down," said Raef, hoping to direct the conversation away from Black Rock. "I can scarcely make out the trees below."

Tup looked over the edge.

"Yes, that would be quite a fall," said the wizard. Tup turned and left Raef at the lip of the mountain. The little man sat on a smooth boulder, facing the villages to the north.

"Come," said Tup, "sit with me."

You crazy old wizard, Raef thought. He shrugged and joined Tup on the rock.

"One of those clearings," Raef said, pointing to the clearings in the trees below, "one of those is Fir Hollow, right?"

Tup nodded.

Raef became uneasy, gazing down over his home village. He felt a sudden urge to go back into the forest below.

"Tell me about your family," said Tup.

"I have an older sister. She was an almoness when I was young, caring for the poor. Now she is married to a mason, so she is no longer an Intercessor. But her husband is of note in the masons guild so she is still well respected."

"I see," said Tup, "Well respected."

"She always was, even as a greenlia. She was known to serve beyond her duties."

"In what way?" asked Tup.

"She would visit the elderly, provide them conversation, and sometimes bring them extra food."

"Seems like an odd way for a greenlia to spend the bit of freedom she would have to spare, after her duties were done."

"We are Intercessors. Our purpose is to serve the village."

"Ah, I see," said Tup, "And your mother. How are you with your mother?"

"I love my mother," said Raef.

Tup's expression became unreadable to Raef, but the older man did not speak. Raef felt the sun begin to warm his back through his shirt. The new sores on his back stung from the heat.

"And your father?" asked Tup, "when you think of him, what is within you?"

"My father is a Keeper, one of the most respected in the village. Even the Prime Keeper defers to my father."

"Yes, but what of you?"

Raef eyed Tup in confusion. "I have great respect for my father. He is the wisest man I know. He is the most learned. He studied in Krellit, with the masters. He is strong and without fear, perhaps more so than the Warriors of Fir Hollow."

"That is not what I asked. What is within you when you think of him?"

Raef's face hardened in frustration, "I have told you. Why do you not listen? I respect my father. I admire him greatly."

Tup cocked his head to one side and his forehead

wrinkled. There was a long silence while Raef tried to determine why this wizard was so easily confused.

"Why is it, Raef, that you cannot say you love your father?"

Raef opened his mouth to speak, to explain how he loved his father. But no words came out. He found he could not say those words. Raef closed his mouth and sat silently on the hard stone.

"Why did you become a Keeper, Raef?"

Why do you change subjects so often? Raef wondered. "Because I had a vision and saw Zul."

"Seeing the Great Spirit does not mean one is destined to become a Keeper," said Tup.

"But, my father is a Keeper."

"Few sons of Keepers become Keepers themselves, Raef. You know this."

"I saw the vision when I had only ten seasons. That is a rare sign, the Prime Keeper told me so. That is when I knew I had to become a Keeper. I told them I was ready."

"You asked to become a Keeper at only ten seasons?" asked Tup.

"Yes! And they took me as an apprentice. I was the only youngling apprentice in Fir Hollow. Perhaps in the entire Province."

Tup shook his head, "An apprentice Keeper before reaching ones thirteenth season. That is quite sad to hear, Raef. I am sorry."

"But…I…I had to become a Keeper! It was my duty, one I was happy to fulfill."

"You had to? In what sense did you have to?"

Raef felt his chest constrict. The air felt suddenly

thinner. "Why are you questioning me like this?" asked Raef, "My village celebrated my choosing!"

"Raef, that is far too great a burden to put on a youngling. Keepers are not chosen until near adulthood. I am sad to hear your village allowed such a thing."

"But my father said…"

"Your father?" interrupted Tup. "This was never about following Zul, was it? That is not who you were trying to impress. Was it?" The wizard's staff began to glow through the cracks in its bark.

Raef looked around, as if for escape, frightened to be so near a wizard and his power.

"You wanted your father's approval more than anything," Tup continued, "but you were never sure you had it."

Raef felt the hairs on his neck stand up. The wizard is right, Raef realized, I do not know how he conjures such understanding, but I know he is right.

"That is where Rail came in," said Tup. "That is where Rail always comes in. Your sister was perfect, at least in your eyes. As a youngling your father was more imposing to you than brilliant. Your mother loved you, but did not protect you. No one knew you, not who you really were. At least, that is what you believed. Rail found you, as Rail always does, and took advantage of all that you feared."

"But Rail did not find me!" said Raef, "I found Rail. I snuck up and watched it in the forest. I was the one who kept coming back."

"Raef, how many seasons did you have when you met Rail?"

"Six seasons."

"And who took you to the dragon?"

"No one, I went alone."

"Raef, no youngling of six seasons goes to meet the dragon alone. It is far too frightening for a youngling to approach. Who introduced you?"

Raef tried to recall. The image of a greenling playing in a hidden meadow came to his mind.

"It was DeAlsím, a greenling in my village. I had seen him with the dragon, way out in the forest. Later he told me he knew the dragon. But it was I who wanted to meet it."

"You asked to see it? You were not afraid?"

Raef's memory was foggy. As he pondered, he recalled how hideous the beast had appeared at first. How oily were its scales. How foul was its breath. How he trembled when he placed his palm against its side.

Why did I do that? Raef wondered, *Why did I place my hand on the dragon when it was so frightening?* Then Raef recalled an earlier memory.

"Wait, that was not the first I saw of Rail!" said Raef; "I remember the dragon chased me across a meadow outside my village. The wind from its wings knocked me to the ground as it flew over me. I was afraid for my life. I ran home to my mother."

Tup raised his eyebrows. "So, if you were afraid of the dragon, why did you go see it?"

"DeAlsím…took me," Raef said, finally remembering, "It was his idea."

Raef waited for Tup to say something, but the wizard remained silent, gazing intently on Raef.

"DeAlsím was a greenling," Raef continued, "yet he did not ignore me. Everyone else pushed me aside, even some of my own friends did. I wanted DeAlsím to like me, so I went with him." Raef felt dampness in his eyes, which embarrassed him greatly. It was hard to continue speaking. "I was afraid. I had forgotten being afraid."

Tup turned to face Raef directly. "Raef, you were deceived. None of this, none, was of your doing. You were young. You were alone. You needed approval from someone, someone greater than you. Rail saw that and sent DeAlsím to lure you to itself, right when you were most vulnerable."

"Rail sent DeAlsím?" asked Raef. It was a stunning revelation. "This…was all the dragon's idea?"

Tup smiled. Raef felt a glimmer of peace, but then shame loomed over him once more.

"But, even so, that excuses nothing," Raef stammered, "I did the same as DeAlsím, when I was and adult. I took Daz, barely a greenling, to see it. To visit the dragon. Daz was my apprentice, my responsibility. And now Daz is at Black Rock. Everyone in Fir Hollow thinks he is dead. But I saw the dragon take him." Raef turned away from the wizard and hung his head, "I am the worst of all. I am a monster, the chief of Dragon Children."

Tup leaned close to Raef. "Raef, listen, this is very important. You are not an evil person. You never have been. I do not believe it is within you to want to hurt anyone. Rail is evil, not you."

Raef turned back to see Tup reach into his robe

and pull out a cloth bag. He loosened the cord and pulled from the bag a large clod of dirt. It was sticky and full of bits of fur, feathers and decaying matter.

"What is that foul thing?" asked Raef.

"This is you," said Tup, "but it is not you. This is how you see yourself—all filth and rot."

Raef looked at the clod of earth, silently agreeing with the wizard's estimation of him.

"But it is not really you." Tup began to pick at the clod, removing bits of earth and decay, the ball growing smaller. "You see, all the dirt is not you, it is what has happened to you. All these bits of ugliness, they have been stuck onto you, but they are not you."

The ball grew smaller as Tup picked off bits of grime. "Much of this," continued the wizard, "Especially these parts down deep, were stuck onto you by Rail. Some by others like DeAlsím and even your father. You added some yourself, of course." Tup looked up and smiled at Raef, "You have rolled in the mud on purpose a few times."

Raef emitted a quick chuckle, feeling dampness grow in his eyes. When the ball became the size of a youngling's fist, Raef saw a glimmer of light blue emerge from under the filth.

"Ah, there you are," said Tup, "that is the real Raef. The Raef Zul sees when he looks at you."

Tup wiped the ball against his sleeve to remove the last bits of earth, and a nearly spherical stone appeared. It was the color of a cloudless sky. Tup held it up to the sun. Light glimmered off its polished surface.

"This, Raef, is you. This is who you were born to

be. The ball of mud that we started with, well, perhaps that may be all anyone can see now. It may be how you appear. But the dirt is not you. The dirt is merely stuck to you. It can be removed. It can be chipped away. Your core is still beneath, unharmed."

Raef stared at the blue ball of stone. It appeared almost magical.

"How? How can it be removed?" asked Raef, "all the dirt?"

"It will take a few seasons," said the old wizard, "after all, it took quite a few seasons to get all that dirt stuck on to you."

A tiny glimmer of hope sparked inside of Raef.

"For now," said Tup, "what I want you to understand is, this is you."

Tup handed the globe to Raef. It felt heavy in his hand as he turned it in the sun. It was polished crystal, and it sparkled in the sun.

This is me? Raef wondered. The thought was too generous, but seemed possibly true. *This is me, not the dirt.*

The wizard stretched. His staff glowed from within.

"Tell me your whole story," said Tup, "start from when Rail chased you in the meadow. Do not fear what I think of you. Remember, I know who you really are inside."

Raef began to unfold his life before the wizard. The secret meetings with Rail in the forest, which grew more frequent as the seasons passed. Introducing his friend, Domik, to the dragon. Taking his younger neighbor, Nilo to see Rail. Becoming an apprentice Keeper, yet continuing to secretly see Rail, even more often than before. Being taken by Rail in the village square, in front of the entire village. Living five seasons at Black Rock, with the other Dragon Children, where he became nothing more than a hollow shell. Returning to his village in shame, only for his village to ignore where he had obviously been, making him a Keeper over them. Betraying the Intercessors and the village by taking his apprentice, Daz, to Rail. Then Rail taking young Daz to Black Rock in front of Raef's eyes. Being discovered by Naan, when she found dragon hairs on his clothing. Then leaving everything in search of the Soul Healer.

Raef was exhausted when he finished, but felt oddly relieved.

"It is nearly dark," said the wizard, "We should return to my hut for last meal."

Raef stood, surprised at how cramped his legs felt. He could scarcely believe he and Tup had been on the mountain an entire sun's journey.

"Return to see me next moon cycle," said Tup as they walked, "Then we will speak more. Until then, I want you to share what you have told me with the other men in Promise."

"In Promise?" said Raef, "I cannot tell them any of this!"

"Just tell them what you are able. They will tell you their stories. It will cause some of the dirt to fall off."

Tup walked down into the trees, vanishing into the shadows. Raef hesitated, took a deep breath, and followed the old wizard.

PART THREE

WINTER DESCENDS

9

Raef woke with a start, shivering uncontrollably. Seven moon cycles had passed since Tup gave Raef the blue stone and winter had come. But this was a cold unlike any Raef had known. He leapt from the mattress and cracked open the shutters to see. Intense light nearly blinded him, causing him to clench his eyes tight. He tried to open them again, but could see nothing other than a painful glare. When his eyes finally adjusted, all he could see was a vast expanse of white, unlike anything he had ever seen. The huts were nearly covered in mounds of snow. The air pouring in was unbearably cold.

"Shut the window!" called Naan from the bed, "it is freezing out there."

Raef closed the shutter and wrapped his night robe tightly around him.

"You could not be more right," he said, "everything is covered in snow. I have never seen so much."

Naan wrapped her robe around her and got up, peaking outside.

"I can scarcely make out the huts," she said, "The snow piled around them nearly reaches the roof on most. I think Ian's hut is completely buried!"

"I had better dress," said Raef.

He collected his clothes from the floor. They were like ice in his fingers. He drew his robe around him tighter at the thought of pulling those over his skin.

"Perhaps we should start a fire and warm up first," he said.

"You start a fire," said Naan, getting back under the covers, "Nine and I will wait here in bed for it to get warm."

Raef grinned at his wife, and then stoked the fire to life. He found it was quite difficult in so much cold. As he coddled the embers he could hear others outside, laughing and joking.

By the time the fire was strong he and Naan had dressed and Nine was fed. Raef peeked outside to see men using hoes to pull snow away from the huts. A couple of greenlings, Evot's sons he was fairly sure, where up on top of Ian's hut, using brooms to sweep snow to the ground. Jesson glanced in Raef's direction and smiled.

"We will be right over to dig you out!" called the young man.

"No, no," called Raef, "I will manage."

Jesson laughed, "How? Your door is completely buried, you will never get out on your own."

Raef sat and strapped on his shoes as he heard digging begin somewhere outside his hut. "Do not worry, Naan, I will get us out," he said.

"Raef," said Naan, "Jesson said they would dig us out. Just have some hot tea with me."

"Naan, I can do this," he said, tugging at the door. It was stuck, so he yanked harder at it. With a loud crack the handle and the a bit of wood it was lashed to broke off, leaving an exposed area where snow show through.

"Raef, come and sit with me," said Naan.

Raef ignored her, sticking his hands through the new hole in the door and wedging his fingers between the snow and the outside of the door. He gave a heave but the door remained frozen shut.

"Why does anyone live out in this frozen waste?" Raef grumbled. He yanked harder against the door and nearly half the door broke off, sending a man-sized pile of snow into their tiny hut.

"Raef, stop it, right now," snapped Naan, "You will burry us all in an avalanche if you keep that up. They will have us out before you know it."

Raef tramped back to his stump and sat. Naan handed him a hot mug of tea. He put it to his lips.

"Ow!" he yelled, as it scalded his tongue. Anger boiled inside of him. He waited, helplessly, to be dug out by the other men.

When Raef was finally free from the snowy prison he went behind his hut to get more firewood. He swept the snow away from the wood pile only to find very little split wood left. He doubted it would last until next sunrise in this weather. His calves were frozen in the deep snow. He sighed. He would have to walk to the barn, where the extra wood was stored, though it contained only un-split logs. Raef began to trudge through the snow, feeling his anger returning.

"How do these people live in this place," he muttered aloud.

Raef looked back to see thick smoke curling up from each hut as men, greenling and older male younglings scurried about clearing snow. No one seemed to notice Raef as he plodded through the unmarked snow over the dormant field.

Apparently everyone else thought to stock up before now, Raef grumbled in his mind, *but, of course, did not bother to warn me of the blizzard that was coming.*

His fingers were frozen blue by the time he returned to his hut with an armful of logs. He dropped them and one fell on his toe.

"Ah!" he whimpered. His deerskin boots were little protection. He would need something better for winter, but he had no idea how to make shoes or boots. It was then that he realized he had nothing to split the wood with.

"Damn the Spirits!" he yelled, kicking at the snow.

Once again Raef trekked through the knee-deep snow, wading to the tool shed. Now and then he stepped into a deep spot, sinking into the powder up to his waist. His clothes had become damp from his sweat and had frozen, making movement difficult. He finally came to the shed where the tools were kept. Raef stopped, staring at the front of the shed where the snow had drifted to nearly his height, completely blocking the door.

"So now I have to dig the door out to get an axe," said Raef to the sky, "Do the spirits hate me?"

The sun was nearing mid sky when he finally

Under the Burning Sun

returned to his hut with and axe. With frozen hands
he put one log on top of another, then lifted the axe.
Just before brining the axe down, the top log fell over,
disappearing into the snow again.

"Ah!" yelled Raef.

He dug out the log and slammed it back on top
of the second log. He lifted the axe and let it fall. The
blade stuck only half a blade deep. He lifted the axe
but the top log came with it, stuck solidly. Raef
pursed his lips and brought the axe and log down hard
against the lower log. The blade moved just a bit
deeper. He lifted the axe, the log firmly attached,
paused, then threw the axe and log against the back
of his hut with a loud bang. Then he turned and
leaned back until his shoulders touched the wall and
slid down to sit in the snow.

"I hate this place!" His voice echoed over the
snow. *Spirits of the Province, what must they think of me?*
He wondered, knowing his voice had echoed
throughout Promise.

He sat in the cold until he began to shiver. Then
very slowly he pulled himself up, took the axe, and
finished splitting the two logs. He decided the other
logs could wait for another sun.

Naan had some thin pottage ready when he got
inside. She did not ask why he had been yelling.

After eating Raef went to find the other men, but
learned they had all gone hunting. Hunting in the
snow? Raef thought, they must be crazy. He trudged
to Tren's hut, knowing the bachelor did not hunt.

"Tren!" called Raef, outside of the bachelor's hut,
"Tren are you home?"

The young man appeared in the doorway, wrapped in a thick robe.

"Raef, what are you doing out there? It is freezing."

"Yes," said Raef, "it is freezing. And I am here to have you join me out in this Spirit forsaken weather."

"What in all the Province for?" asked Tren.

"It is mid sun," said Raef, "a bit past, actually, and while it may be cold, there are no clouds and the sun is out."

Tren's face looked puzzled.

"Tren," said Raef with impatience, "mid sun...it is time."

Tren's face resolved into understanding, "You... you want us to go to purging?"

Raef nodded, "The other's have gone hunting, or some such thing, and will likely purge out there. But we are still here."

"I was sort of planning on passing, due to the snow and all," said Tren.

"I think we are supposed to do it anyway," said Raef.

With much huffing and complaining, Tren changed clothes and joined Raef for the slow walk through the snow. No one was outside any longer; they were all tucked in to their warm huts. Tren did not speak all the way to the purging field.

The icy air slapped Raef's back the instant he removed his shirt.

"Ghah!" said Tren, as his coat and shirt fell away, "I hate the winter!"

"I m...m...must agree with you, friend,"

stammered Raef. Then a new blister burst on Raef's back and searing heat sizzled his skin where the sunlight touched liquid essence.

"Uhn!" cried Raef. The mixture of freezing and boiling all at once was nearly unbearable.

"Now do you see why I did not want to come?" asked Tren.

"Yes," Raef grunted, "but do we not have to do this anyway?"

"I suppose," said Tren, "But when it is this cold I sometimes do not participate in purging."

Raef trembled silently in the bitter air. *Is it permissible to miss a purging or two?* He wondered. He did not know, as this was still new to him. Just to be safe, Raef insisted they stay as long as was normal, though he found it difficult.

Raef accompanied Tren to his hut afterward.

"Come in for a bit, Raef," said Tren.

Raef entered the small hut and looked around. It was very clean, more so than most. A curtain hung over one wall, something Raef remembered from when He and Naan had stayed with Tren upon arriving in Promise.

Tren must have seen Raef staring as he walked to the curtain and pulled it aside. Behind were floor to ceiling shelves of elaborately carved stone bowls, cups and other containers.

"Tren, this is amazing," said Raef. "Did you make all of them?"

"Yes," said Tren, "I carve mainly in winter, but I am always working on something new." He picked a black goblet from a shelf and handed it to Raef.

"It is heavy," said Raef.

"It is carved from black granite," said Tren, "Of course it is heavy."

"I have never seen anything so…so fancy. Not even in Midland."

"Midland?" asked Tren.

"The city of trade," explained Raef.

"Well, we do not trade with anyone," said Tren, "so I just give them away. We may be isolated out here, but we eat with the dinnerware of kings." Tren smiled, holding up a royal-looking goblet.

"I see that you do," said Raef, admiring the rows of ornate carvings. "I wish I could do something like this. It seems I have nothing much to offer anyone, even out here in Promise."

"Sure you do," said Tren, "you work in the fields with me!"

Raef smiled at the man. It was a nice sentiment, but Raef knew it was not really a compliment. It made sense why Tren did not mind working in the fields with the women and greenlias. He had something special, something no one else could do. Raef had nothing. Raef stayed for a mug of ale, then returned home.

After last meal Raef sat by the fire holding a mug of tea. Nine crawled to his side and giggled at him. He tussled her hair and picked her up, putting her into his lap.

I am trying, he thought to himself, *I am really trying, but…what will I ever amount to?*

Raef stared into the fire and before long was somewhere else. Some place where it was not cold and where he was a person of note.

Around him the air felt slightly damp but it was warm. He was flying, his arms out to his sides as he rose and fell through the sky. His legs were wrapped around the neck of a graceful flying beast. He was with Rail, flying circles through the thin mist above the ancient caldera that was Black Rock.

10

Raef waited with Ramey near the lodge for Siro and Evot to join them. Raef had wrapped his boots with another layer of leather and bound it with straps. He hoped they would hold together for the trip. Siro and Evot emerged from beyond the other end of the settlement, carrying a bow and some weapons Raef was not familiar with. Raef did not recall seeing weapons in the tool hut or barn. Perhaps they had been stored in the stable, he rarely had reason to go there.

"I was hoping you would join us eventually," said Siro.

"Yes, good to have you along," said Evot, holding a bow and quiver or arrows out to Raef, "These are my son's weapons. He said you could use them until you can make your own."

Raef accepted the gift. "I have little choice," he said, "We have used up our ration of meat."

"You will do fine," said Siro, "This is a short trip, only one sun's journey."

"That is why I am finally coming," said Raef, "I

am not quite ready to sleep out in the snow."

"We will probably only see rabbits this close in," said Ramey.

"That is fine," said Raef, "Rabbits are the only things I have actually ever killed before." He shuddered at the memory.

Even with his long legs, Raef found it difficult to keep up as the men tread briskly through the snow. Raef lost his sense of direction entirely before the sun reached one-quarter sky. The men were not speaking, which made Raef uncomfortable. He decided to ask about something he had overheard around the fire.

"Is it true?" asked Raef, "Did Tren really visit Rail a few suns back?"

"Yes, it is sadly true," said Evot. "Two suns past. He did not admit it to us until sunrise past. He is with Ian, walking up to see Tup as we speak."

"But, how?" asked Raef, "How could that happen?"

"He went off on his own," said Siro, "which is never wise."

"But, has Tren not lived here in Promise many seasons?" asked Raef, "Is he not strong enough yet to travel alone?"

"What is so important about traveling alone?" asked Ramey.

Am I forever to require a traveling companion? Raef wondered. *Will I be trapped like some prisoner who requires a constant guard?*

"Sh! Quiet," whispered Siro, "We have arrived."

Siro and Evot left Ramey and Raef behind a fallen log and walked off somewhere in the woods.

Ramey seemed to be able to fold nicely into a compact position, barely visible behind the log, but Raef's long legs made it difficult.

Raef tried to keep still but his legs began to cramp and his toes lost their feeling due to the cold. He ached to move. When he began to shiver he rubbed his hands together to warm them. Ramey held his finger to his lips. Raef nodded and tried tucking his hands under his coat.

After what seemed like an eternity, Raef noticed Ramey was moving. The young man drew his bow so slowly Raef had to blink to be sure he was moving. Ramey rotated the tip of his arrow to point to their left. Raef squinted in the direction the arrow pointed but could see nothing but trees and snow. He had just begun to make out a spot under the dry limbs of a bush that was moving when the thwack of Ramey's bowstring broke the silence. Raef startled as the distant spot jumped. It was a rabbit, an arrow protruding from its side. Ramey launched across the frozen ground as the little animal kicked against the powdery snow. The young man snatched it off the ground, drew his knife and slit its neck. A flow of steaming crimson stained the snow as Ramey held the rabbit by its legs. Ramey waited for the blood to stop and used his boot to cover the spot in snow before returning to hide next to Raef.

"Sometimes they squeal," whispered Ramey, "so it is good to silence them so other animals don't hear and run. We may get one or two more here if we can keep quiet."

Raef tentatively lifted his own bow over the log

to be ready when another rabbit came. He found it very difficult to keep his focus on the forest around him. His mind wandered easily and his legs cramped.

Just after mid sun Raef heard the swoosh of Ramey's arrow again. Raef turned to see Ramey dash off to his right and snag another rabbit. They did not see another.

Siro and Evot returned just before three quarter sun, each carrying several rabbits. Ramey stood up and stretched, so Raef did as well. His legs ached.

"How did you get so many?" Raef asked the older men.

"Excellent eyesight," said Evot, with a grin.

"And I can hit a rabbit a hundred spans away," said Siro.

Ramey began to laugh, "Do not listen to either of them. They were collecting kills from traps they set out sunrise last."

"Oh," said Raef, feeling slightly less useless.

"We should eat something," said Siro.

Evot opened a bag of dried meat and bread. It was spiced venison jerky that Garma was known for. The men began to joke and laughed as they ate.

"Are you not worried we will scare the rabbits away?" asked Raef.

"We will move to another spot after we eat," said Siro.

After eating Raef followed the men to another spot. He found it distressingly difficult to keep up with them, especially as all but Ramey were older men. Once in place, all four remained together, behind boulders and trees not far apart. Raef did spot two rabbits. The first sprung away before he could lift his bow. He did manage to get an arrow off at the second rabbit, but he missed it completely. Ramey killed it before it got away.

"The sun is low," said Evot, "And we had better head back before it is dark."

Raef stood wearily with the others, feeling almost too frozen to move. On the way back, he began to worry about what he would tell Naan. They had not eaten meat in half a moon cycle.

Evot held his hand up and all the men stopped. A tiny clearing in the tree was just ahead. Unlike most of the forest, this clearing had obvious animal tracks all through the snow. The men found places to hide, Raef behind a tall stump.

Then Raef saw it, a rabbit, and a fairly large one. It was digging in the snow at the opposite edge of the clearing. Raef slowly pointed his bow and drew back the bowstring. He found it hard to keep his aim steady.

The rabbit was a bit farther than Raef would have liked. He pulled his bowstring back a bit farther and hoped for the best. He released the arrow and the rabbit sat up and looked at him. The rabbit bolted and the arrow struck just behind it. Raef was certain he missed, but the rabbit fell to its stomach and thrashed its back legs in the snow. The arrow had stuck in its hind leg.

The rabbit stumbled upright, arrow still in its leg, and began a staggered hop that was surprisingly quick. Raef fumbled to find another arrow and string it in his bow. He stood and shot again, but missed entirely this time. Just before the rabbit was out of range another arrow hit it square in the back and it fell to its side. Raef looked over to see Evot standing with his bow.

"Go get it," said Evot, "it is yours."

Raef ran to the rabbit, drew his knife and killed it quickly. The other men came to his side as he removed the arrows. He gave one back to Evot.

"I was not the one who killed it," said Raef.

"It would not have lived," said Evot. "I was just helping a little. You could have chased it down in its condition, I was just saving you that trouble."

Raef held up the rabbit to look at.

"A big one," said Ramey, "well done!"

Raef tried to smile for the others, but could not. Evot deserved this rabbit, but Raef knew his family needed it. He nodded his agreement.

It was a long walk back to Promise and Raef felt half-frozen when he finally entered his own hut.

"Well, this is all I got," said Raef, holding up his kill as he entered.

Naan turned to him as he entered.

"A rabbit!" she said, "Oh, good. I was not sure what you were hunting. I was afraid you would come back with a squirrel. Rabbit is much better, and this is a large one."

Raef exhaled in relief at his wife's approval and handed her the animal.

"It is only one," he said.

"But it will last two or three suns," said Naan. "I am happy you went."

Naan insisted Raef wash up and rest by the fire

while she prepared last meal. She even had hot tea prepared for him. He saw little Nine sleeping on their mattress. The baby twitched as if she were dreaming. Naan came to his side and put a hand on his shoulder.

"She would not take a nap at all so she fell asleep early. I think she was trying to stay awake until you came home."

Raef watched his daughter roll to her back and grab at the air with her tiny hands.

Naan and Nine deserve better than me, thought Raef, *Everyone is trying to make me feel better, but I cannot do anything right. I am no good at this…at anything. I am going to end up like Tren, a Dragon Child who never heals.*

Raef felt his wife's hand on his arm. He tried to gain comfort from her touch, but comfort did not come to him.

11

Raef threw his head back against the straw mattress as Nine fussed and cried on the floor.

"Mother will be home next sun," said Raef.

Nine leaned forward, pressing her face to the earthen floor, and cried. Raef sighed and pulled himself up, then crawled to his daughter, picking her up and hugging her. She leaned back and flailed her arms and screamed louder. Naan had been gone two suns already, up the mountain to see the wizard.

"That is all I can take," said Raef, to no one in particular, "we are going to Jesson's. At least there your cries will be drown out by other the younglings."

Raef stood and wrapped a blanket around himself and his daughter. She became quiet when Raef opened the door. The wind cut through his clothing like a knife. He stepped outside and snow found its way through the many holes in his deteriorating boots. Raef hugged Nine's small face to his chest as he pushed through knee-high snow. Jesson's hut was just to the left of his own. Raef paused in front of the door to announce his presence.

"Jesson! This is Raef, coming to call!"

The door opened and Jesson peeked his head out. "Raef," said the man, "Get inside! Don't stand outside calling in this weather. Just come in!"

Raef pushed inside and stamped the snow from his boots.

"You need new shoes," said Jesson, looking down at Raef's feet.

"I am no cordswainer," said Raef, "and I have no leather even if I were."

"Ura and Wynn make most of our boots," said Jesson, "you only need ask."

"Perhaps Naan can make some," Raef said, "She has learned to sew clothing. Perhaps it is similar."

"Raef," said Jesson, "I am serious. Ura and Wynn would both be happy to help."

Three younglings jammed themselves between Raef and Jesson, interrupting the conversation.

"You be Reef, right?" said one small female.

"His calling is Raef," said Jesson.

"It is Raef, smelly, not Reef," said a slightly taller male, slapping the smaller female on the arm.

"Do not strike your sister," said Jesson, but the smaller youngling had already begun a full-scale assault on her older brother, both hands flailing at him.

"Stop it, stop it!" said the older brother, "Daddy, see what she is doing?"

"I do believe you started…" Jesson began, but was tackled from behind by two other younglings. They giggled as they tried to wrestle their father to the ground.

"Come sit," said the young woman who was Jesson's wife, motioning to Raef.

Raef stepped around the throng and made his way to a bench, tripping over wooden toys on the floor. Nine squirmed in his arms, wriggling her arms toward a baby on the floor. Raef sat and put Nine on the floor, who scooted rapidly to the other baby. The baby sat up and squealed at Nine.

"Zishi always loves to see Nine," said the woman.

Raef struggle to remember Jesson's wife's calling.

Nine crawled to Zishi and the two began to giggle and hug each other.

"Naan is still up seeing Tup?" asked Jesson, who came to sit next to Raef.

"Yes. She was gone sunrise past and will return at sunset tomorrow. I keep Nine down here with me, now that she is a bit older. To make it easier for Naan."

Jesson's wife stood and walked to the central fire, stirring the coals.

"You look a bit ragged," Jesson said to Raef.

Raef held his hands out toward the fire. "I am not used to caring for Nine so long," said Raef, "Three suns alone are much longer with a baby."

"It is only fair," said Jesson's wife, "Naan watches Nine when you are gone, and you can hardly expect her to carry Nine all the way up the mountain in this weather."

"Yes, yes," said Raef.

Jesson laughed and slapped Raef on the back.

"Do not be glum, my friend," said Jesson.

"But I just sit in the hut, sun after sun, doing

nothing. Too cold to go outside or even keep the windows open. How do you stand the dark?"

The two oldest of Jesson's younglings, both males, chased each other in circles. One tripped and tumbled into Raef, landing on his lap. The youngling rolled to his back, looked up at Raef and smiled, then ran off after his brother, growling like an animal. Jesson looked into Raef's eyes and began to smile. Raef cringed at the noise of high-pitched voices.

"You do not like all this commotion, do you?"

"Your children are wonderful," said Raef, accepting a mug of ale Jesson's wife handed him. He brought it to hip lips, only for his hand to be yanked away by a small youngling who had jumped up to hang from his arm. Ale spilled on the little female's head but she only hung on and grinned at Raef.

"Here, come play with your brothers," said Jesson, pulling the youngling away.

Raef took a rapid drink, keeping a keen eye out for attacking younglings.

"You should come hunting with us," said Jesson, "We will be going again soon, and I know you must need meat."

"My last trip with Ramey, Ian and Siro did not go well."

"You can learn, can you not?"

Raef shrugged. He recalled the last trip through the icy forest, his fingers freezing as he held a bowstring. He shivered and drank more ale.

"How is Naan adjusting to Promise?" asked the woman.

Raef tried again to remember her calling.

"Sir Raef," said a young male, "do you want to see my arm muscles?"

"Wait until you taste Siro's venison jerky," said Jesson, "It is the food of spirits."

"Oh, Raef, I am sorry but one of my younglings stepped on Nine's fingers," said the woman, handing a crying Nine to Raef.

"Why are your boots so torn like that, sir Raef?"

"Why did you call your baby 'Nine'?"

"Here, look at the new bow I carved. See how bendy it is?"

"Did Naan tell you she sewed my new dress?"

"Sir, Raef…sir Raef, why is your hair so long?"

"Does everyone have long hair in your village?"

"My dad says you were an innesessor. What is an innesessor?"

Raef put his mug on the table and pulled Nine to his chest. He held her little hand to his lips and kissed her finger. Her crying diminished.

"I think I need to get Nine to bed now," said Raef. "Thank you for your company."

Raef trudged through the snow to his hut. He removed his clothing and put on his sleeping robe, though the sun was still far from setting. He hugged Nine and reclined on his stump. His clothes were unfolded on the floor. An unwashed kettle sat on the table, next to his unwashed spoon and knife. The fire was nearly out. Nine began to cry again. Raef closed his eyes and imagined he was in Black Rock.

Erif walked down the beach alone. The breeze

was weak, the sun was hot, and his skin was cracked.

"I miss you, Tama," Erif said out loud. "And my younglings—I do not even know what they would look like by now. This is a high price to pay, for all of us."

"You are lonely today," said a voice that made Erif jump.

"Zul! Do not sneak up on me like that."

"I am sorry to surprise you, old friend."

"Yes, I am lonely. But…I am missing my wife and family, more than usual."

"I cannot change that now," said Zul, "it is not yet time."

"I know," said Erif. He looked out to sea, tears escaping his eyes.

"I have not left you here completely alone," said Zul. "It is not the same, I understand, but it is something."

Erif turned to ask the spirit what he meant, but Zul was already fading. As the spirit vanished, a sleek, bounding ball of fur appeared over a grassy dune, running directly toward Erif.

"Well, girl, where have you been?"

The coyote joined him, running circles around him. Erif smiled down at the small beast.

"Well," said Erif, "You are not human, but it is good to have you here."

The coyote looked up at him and whined.

"Yes, it is very good."

12

Raef opened the door for his wife, elated to finally see her again.

"Is there anything to eat?" asked Naan, as she came into the hut and shed her snow-covered coat.

"Of course," said Raef, "I left the pottage over the fire so it is still warm."

Raef put Naan's frozen coat and boots in a corner.

Nine squealed and Naan picked her up.

"My little baby!" said Naan, "I missed you so much!"

"And I missed you," said Raef, coming to join the hug.

Naan pulled away and moved to sit at the table.

"Here, try this," said Raef, spooning pottage into a rock carved bowl.

"What is in this?" she asked, taking a spoon full, "it is rather bland."

"I used potato, I know you like that. We are out of salt, though."

"And we are out of meat as well I see," said

Naan.

"Naan, you knew we were almost out when you left for the mountain."

Naan continued to eat slowly.

"How was your time with Tup?" asked Raef.

"It was freezing."

"Yes, here as well. But how was Tup? What did you think?"

Naan slammed her spoon to the table and glared at Raef.

"Do you really want to know what I am thinking? I am thinking I would not be in this frozen waste if it were not for you. I am thinking my feet would not feel like they are being stabbed with a hundred needles after a full sun's journey through the snow. I am wondering what you have been doing since I was gone. Did you take care of Nine? She is filthy. Did you go looking for that dragon? You certainly did nothing to clean the hut. Did you run off with your dragon friends and tell stories of how wonderful it was at Black Rock?"

"Naan!" said Raef, "I do not do those things any longer, and you know that."

"Do I? Raef, you lied to me for how many seasons before I found a dragon hair in your clothes? Why should I trust you now?"

Raef stammered, but had no answer for her.

Nine began to whimper.

"And am I happy to be home?" Naan continued, "I really do not know. This hut is tiny. I cannot take three steps without having to turn around. I am still trying to find work to help us earn food. I sew, even though I never wanted to be seamstress. All the while you mope here in the hut from sunrise to sunset, pouting that you are not treated special like you were in Fir Hollow."

Naan stood to face Raef and he took a step back.

"Well, Raef, you are not special here. You are just like everyone else. And perhaps you should get outside and work like everyone else too. Or shall your family starve while you are waiting for someone to feel sorry for you?"

Raef stood in silence. Naan left her half-finished pottage on the table and picked up Nine and began to prepare for bed. Raef silently cleaned up the food.

13

"You should not go alone," Naan said.

Raef slung a bow over his shoulder; one that Jesson had helped him carve. Naan had sewn the quiver and Siro helped him make the arrows.

"The other men are out on a long hunt," he replied, "they may not be back for several suns. We will run out of meat before then. Besides, Zul will protect me. I trust Zul."

Raef stepped out into the snow. He smiled to himself. He was a hunter now. Raef left the circle of huts, heading into the forest alone as the sun broke the horizon. It was an unusually cloudless sky.

Now if I can only keep from getting lost out here.

It had snowed twice since the other men had left. There was no trace of their tracks.

That is okay, he thought, *if I followed them I would only be going where the game has already been scared off or hunted out.*

Raef inhaled deeply, exhaling steam into the air. The tension from being cooped up in a tiny hut floated away with his breath. He did not even mind his frozen feet.

As the sun approached mid sky Raef continued pushing through the snow. He had never been this far out in the forest since coming to Promise.

I am still not sure about that wizard, Raef thought.

He heard the scatter of little paws on frozen snow but did not pause. Certainly the best game lay further from the scent of man. Perhaps he might even find a deer, if he walked far enough.

He saw the green tips of fern poking up through the snow and walked toward them. Raef paused, moving his fingers over the delicate fronds. Something about the fern brought him comfort.

It is so nice to be out here, he thought, *So nice to be away from the other voices.* Raef closed his eyes briefly and raised his face to soak in the weak rays of sun.

A faint scent floated in the air that made Raef's heart race and his skin tingle. He wasn't sure what it was but it was familiar and made him instantly happy. He opened his eyes and ran forward.

Raef brushed aside a thin curtain of fir branches then froze in his tracks. He was standing at the edge of a small meadow, a circle of unbroken snow. His bow slid from his shoulder and dropped to the snow. He raised his head, looking up the looming figure opposite him across the meadow. The green orbs of Rail's eyes peered down on him.

"It has been so long," the dragon's baratone voice resonated.

Raef paused briefly, feeling conflict with in him, before running to the dragon.

The sun was low in the sky when Raef finally

returned to Promise. Raef paused at the circle of huts as he approached. No one was outside.

I should just run away, he thought, *I am no good for this place.*

Raef reached behind himself and touched his neck. It was wet. He held his hand to his face. It glistened with saliva.

More essence to purge, he realized. "Damn!" he muttered, "Damn the Spirits!"

Raef blinked back tears and looked across the circle to his own hut. A thin trail of smoke rose from its roof. Naan was in there, with Nine, probably ready for him and last meal.

This will kill her, he thought. Raef took a deep breath and walked to his hut.

"This is hard to watch," said Erif, staring down into the pool of water. Raef could still be seen trudging through the snow."

"It is no easier for I," said Zul.

"Zul, what if…what if I fail someday? What if I let down my wife and younglings? What if I disgrace myself somehow?"

Zul's arm went around the Warrior.

"Have I ever abandoned Raef?" asked Zul. "Even after all his failures?"

14

Raef stood shirtless in the frozen air, his back bent to the distant sun. His arms shivered, covered in goose bumps. His neck and back burned and sizzled under the sun.

"We have to stay a bit longer," said Ian, "to rid more of the new essence."

Raef grimaced from pain more severe than he had felt in many moon cycles. The other men had dressed and all but Ian and Siro gone back to their huts. Raef wished they would leave too, so he could suffer alone.

"You could have asked for help," said Siro, "we would have come with you."

Raef did not respond. *What can I possibly say? They are wasting their time with me. I am beyond hope.*

"This is not a journey you can make alone," said Siro.

"None of us can," said Ian.

"You are not like me," said Raef, "I may not have gone to Black Rock until I entered my thirteenth season, but I was a dragon lover since I had only six seasons."

"Is that what you think?" asked Siro, "that you are worse than us because you befriended the dragon with so few seasons?"

Raef felt his chest tighten and his lips quiver. "That is nothing," he replied, "I brought a youngling to the dragon. More than one. Rail did not need to seek out new children, I brought them to it. And I was a Keeper."

Raef trembled in the cold.

Siro and Ian came closer to Raef, who was still bent over under the sun. Siro put a hand on Raef's shoulder. Raef shook uncontrollably and his breathing became ragged.

"So this is it," said Siro, "you are so much worse than the rest of us that we cannot help you."

Raef tried to respond but found he was too close to weeping. He remained silent.

"You do not know my story, do you Raef?" asked Siro, "I think it is time you hear it."

Siro did not release Raef's shoulder.

"I have no memory of when I did not know Rail," said Siro, "My parents had befriended the dragon seasons before I was born. We lived near the village of Crest Ridge. Rail had a secret place there, as it does near all villages, but my parents lived in the hidden meadow. We lived outdoors like animals, without even a hut.

"Others came to join us when Rail visited. My family were the dragon lovers of Crest Ridge. I can vaguely remember going into the village from time to time, when I was very small, and not being allowed to mention the dragon. But I did. I told other younglings like me. Some would come and find us and I would show them the dragon.

"My parents were taken by Rail when I had only eight seasons. I was confused and afraid. I thought it was punishing me for not loving it enough. I thought that is why it took them and not me. But two or three suns later Rail returned and flew me to Black Rock."

"I did not know you were so young," said Raef, "when you knew Rail."

"Black Rock did not frighten me," said Siro, "I have heard others tell of how shocking Black Rock was when they first arrived. But to me, well, I had always lived outdoors, covered in filth. In Black Rock everyone was like me. Everyone else was finally like me.

"That was not the hard part. My parents were the hard part. They had never paid much attention to me before, but at least we were always within eyesight at all times. In Black Rock they wandered far and wide, never bothering to come find me, or even each other for that matter. They abandoned me, which only drew me closer to Rail. I never parted the dragon's side when it was in the Great Basin."

Raef began to take deep uneven breaths, fighting back a wave that was trying to overtake him. He dared to gaze into Siro's eyes. *Siro has more scars than any of us,* Raef realized, *not a spot on his back that is unmarred. Now I know why.*

"We are like you," said Ian, coming to Raef's other side, "You are not different."

Raef finally began to sob.

15

Raef emerged from his hut to the glare of bright sunlight. He was surprised to see more than half of Promise gathered around Evot's hut. He walked across the circle to see a gaping hole in the roof. Evot's family were outside, wrapped in blankets, obviously having left the hut before dressing properly.

"Caved in just before sunrise," said Evot as Raef came to his side, "I am a bit surprised. It has always held the snow before."

Raef looked at the deep snow covering all the hut roofs.

"It has snowed every sunset all moon cycle," said Raef, "but it gets warmer by mid sun."

Ian came to join them.

"I think the wet snow is causing new snow to stick more," Raef continued, "Rather than simply blow off in the wind."

"You make a good argument," said Ian.

"We should probably all remove the excess snow from our roofs," said Raef.

Evot sighed, "The young man is right. We used to

shovel our roofs each winter but have gotten lazy over the seasons."

"Well, looks like we have our work cut out for us!" said Ian.

"I can help," said Raef, "Back in my village we had several roofs collapse like this. I supervised the repairs."

Well, not supervise how the work was done, Raef admitted to himself, *but I was charged with seeing to it the workers did the repairs. And I watched enough to see how it was done. I can do this, I am certain of it.*

"Excellent," said Ian, "you lead the way."

Raef sent Evot's eldest sons to cut saplings to replace the structural poles.

"Be sure to find the straightest ones you can," he told them, "and they must be the length of both of you together to be long enough."

"And you," said Raef to a greenling son of Ian, "fetch the saw from the shed." The greenling dashed through the snow toward the shed.

"Ramey," continued Raef, "You and Jesson go find some mud."

"That might be hard as cold as it as been," said Jesson.

"We can work it until it thaws," said Ramey, "I think I know a place where we may find some."

"The hardest will be finding dead grass," said Raef, "as most will be soft or rotten by now."

"We will go and see what we can find," said Evot's wife, Garma, "and I will take some women and my daughters to help."

Raef climbed to the roof while the supplies were

being gathered. Being tall and slim made climbing easy. Inspecting the hole in the roof, he could see that the mud used to hold the roof together had become too wet. *Probably from melting snow,* he decided. *Then the grass and sticks just fell apart, or had become rotten with age.* He noticed three of the structural poles had broken as well. *Ah,* he thought, *now that was from the excess weight of snow.*

Raef took hold of one of the broken poles and tugged on it. Then he pulled harder until the entire pole came loose. He tossed it to the ground and tugged the second broken pole.

"Are you certain you should remove that?" asked Ian.

"It is better to replace the entire pole replace just the broken section," said Raef.

"But, will not the roof become too weak without it?" asked Evot.

"It should be fine for a short time," said Raef.

Raef pulled the second pole free. The section above the hole sagged a little. Raef inspected the sagging section. *I think it will hold,* he reasoned, *there are still sticks running side to side to hold up the snow.*

Raef tugged at the third broken pole.

"Raef!" came Evot's voice, "the roof is giving way!"

Raef stood, straddling the hole each foot braced on either side against an unbroken pole. He heaved the remaining broken pole upward, hoping to pull the sagging section back up. He watched as the snow sunk further and further down, in spite of his efforts.

"Argh!" grunted Raef, as he pulled harder.

The pole in his hand broke at the crown of the roof and Raef fell forward. He grasped at the smaller sticks to keep from falling through the hole. His feet slipped and he fell face first into the sagging section of roof, above the hole.

"Raef, get off the roof!" came a man's voice.

Raef rose back up, planted each foot on a solid pole, took two handfuls of sticks and grass from the sagging section, and leaned back to pull up as hard as he could. Two loud cracks rang out and Raef felt the roof give way under him.

"Raef!" called out a voice he knew belonged to his wife.

Then he fell. The entire roof seemed to fall with him. Raef found himself on his back, staring up at the blue sky, surrounded by snow and broken sticks. The hole above him now engulfed half of Evot's roof.

Raef sat up. All that had been inside Evot's hut was covered in snow. Then more snow from what was left of the roof above slid down and covered Raef.

Two pair of arms came through the snow and pulled him out. He dare not look to see who had freed him, staring at the ground as he emerged from the ruined hut. Evot came to his side, along with several of his younglings.

"I…I am so sorry," said Raef.

No one spoke and Raef finally looked up. Every member of Promise now surrounded him. Ian was looking at the ground, rubbing the back of his neck. Evot glanced at Raef, and then looked at his hut.

"We…we will need to dig out our belongings," said Garma, "Perhaps we can take everything to the storage barn and clean it up there."

One of Evot's younglings, a small female, began to cry.

Raef stood motionless in the freezing snow.

16

Erif tapped a rock carefully against a crude nail to fasten the last piece of wood on the box he was making for Tama. He had no real tools to work with and the nails he had fashioned from bits of iron. He was making a decorative wooden box for Tama to keep her most precious things in. He wanted to come home with something for her. The nail was not entering the wood easily so he struck it harder. The wood split open, shattering it and another sidepiece it dovetailed into.

"Argh!" Erif said as he tossed the rock off to one side.

He looked down at the box. *It is ruined,* he thought. *I've worked eight suns already on this.*

Erif tried to slow his breathing. He realized his fists were tight. He slowly relaxed them. He stepped away and looked towards the beach.

"Is it really that bad?"

Erif turned to see Zul and smiled.

"Probably not."

Erif walked back and picked up the small box, turning it an examining every side.

"I have another full season out here on this island," said Erif, "Even if I have to remake the entire thing, that is okay."

"Is there enough wood left to rebuild it," asked Zul.

Erif laughed, "Are you trying to make me angry?"

"Are you angry?"

Erif sat in the sand and laughed, "You can be cruel sometimes."

The Great Spirit sat next to Erif in the sand and took the box.

"This would be a nice gift to your wife," said Zul, "If you can finish it, that is."

Erif leaned back on his hands, "I half want to yell at you, and I half want to laugh."

"You may do both if you like," said the spirit.

"Why is this so hard to get past?" asked Erif.

The old spirit smiled and handed the box back to Erif.

"I will have to remove the last two pieces I put on," Erif said, examining his creation, "and maybe use a different kind of wood, because this is all gone. It may not look as nice as I hoped."

"Imperfection is okay with me," said Zul.

"And it will be with Tama as well," said Erif. "I think I will take a walk on the beach. I need a break from all this tedious work."

"Am I allowed to come with you?" asked Zul.

"I was hoping you would."

Raef sat by the fire in Tup's hut, holding a mug of tea. The scent of wet sod drifted through the window. He was finding it hard to look at the old man directly.

"I really messed up back in Promise," said Raef.

"Really? In what way?"

"I was helping Evot fix his roof and I broke it instead."

"Yes…"

"I destroyed his roof rather than fix it and ruined everything inside his hut in the process."

Raef had a strong urge to leave and go walk alone in the forest.

"So," said the wizard, "what should you do next time?"

"I do know how to fix a roof," Raef said, "Next time I need to remove all the snow before I start pulling at broken poles."

"Well, perhaps, but what if you still do not fix it correctly?"

"Remove the grass and sticks before trying to replace a main pole that goes under them," said Raef, "That is what they did back in Fir Hollow. How could I not remember that? That was really…so very stupid of me not to do."

"But what if you do ruin another roof?"

"I…I just need to be more careful. Work more slowly."

"But if you ruin it even when doing all of those things?" asked Tup.

"I should not break a roof I am trying to repair, especially someone else's roof."

"But what if you do?" asked Tup.

Raef stood up and slammed his mug down on the table, "What do you want me to say? I already admitted I need to do better next time."

"Better?" asked Tup, cocking his head and smiling, "Why do you need to do better?"

Raef raised his arms and shook his head. "What are you saying?"

"Raef," said Tup, "if you break someone else's roof again, it is okay."

"What?"

"It is okay. It is okay to be wrong. It is okay to fail. It is okay to not be good enough."

Raef tumbled to his seat. Memories of his father yelling at him came to mind. Yelling at him for breaking something or not doing a task well enough.

"It is okay to fail," said Tup. "I accept you, as a friend, after you fail. Everyone in Promise accepts you when you fail. But even if none of us do, Zul accepts you when you fail."

"I…I do not know," mumbled Raef.

We do not befriend you because of how good you are. We accept you because we like you. Failures and all. The question is, can you accept yourself when you fail?"

17

It was late spring as Raef neared Tup's hut. The sun was only three quarters sky. Raef smiled to himself. This journey once took a full sun to complete.

"Take it easy," Siro huffed behind him, "I do not have your youth."

"I am not so young, old man," said Raef.

"Oh…oh, you wait," said Siro, "I am telling Tup about that remark!"

Raef paused for Siro, but did not hold back a laugh.

"Ah, my friends," came a familiar voice.

Raef turned to see the wizard standing beside the trail between two large trees.

"You arrived early," said Tup.

"That is because Raef thinks this is a race," said Siro, "he has obviously learned nothing of patience from you."

Tup smiled, "Well, Siro, you can rest with me. Raef, go on up to the top. Zul is waiting for you."

"In your hut?" asked Raef.

"Not my hut," said Tup, "the summit."

"Zul…wants to see me?" said Raef, "Alone?"

The wizard nodded, then turned to Siro and began talking.

Raef shook his head, and then continued on to the summit alone. When he arrived, the ancient spirit was waiting. Raef was shocked to see the Great Spirit in solid form, standing as a normal man before him.

"You have arrived," said Zul.

"Zul, you are…"

"Real?" Zul asked with an amuzed expression.

"No, I mean," Raef said, feeling embarrassed, "I just never saw you before…like this."

Zul smiled.

"You…wanted to see me?" asked Raef.

Zul pointed to the eastern ledge. Raef crept slowly across the summit, noticing the clouds had become thick. Even as he walked, a fog began to envelop the mountain top, so dense Raef could scarcely make out the edge of the mountain.

He approached cautiously, remembering that it ended abruptly and dropped off in a shear cliff. He paused, peering down. He could see nothing but fog below him. Realizing he could not hear the Great Spirit, Raef looked behind him. The spirit was gone.

Raef spun around at the sound of a voice coming from an impossible direction.

"Come."

It sounded like Zul, but the voice came from somewhere out beyond the mountain.

"Come where? I am at the very edge already."

"Come," said the voice again.

Raef craned his neck in all directions. Perhaps

there was a path he had not noticed before that lead down this side of the mountain. He saw none. The formless voice continued to call to him from out in the mist.

"I cannot see you," said Raef.

There was no answer, only the repeating call, which was now slowly growing farther away.

"I cannot come," said Raef. "I would die if I step off this mountain."

"Come."

"What are you saying?" asked Raef, as he eased forward until the toes of his boots hung over the edge of the cliff. "Are you...are you asking me to step off?"

"Come."

Raef's hard began to race. "I...I cannot."

"You want to be free from the dragon?" said Zul's voice, "Then you must come."

"I am not strong enough. Not to do what you are asking."

"It is the only path to freedom."

"Through mid air?" asked Raef. "I cannot walk on air."

"Of course you cannot. Do you trust me?"

"I...I do not know."

"That is the first honest thing you have said since you have come to Promise."

The air began to grow cold. Raef closed his eyes and his body began to tremble.

"Come," said Zul, "There is only one path away from the dark spirit, anything else is a waste of your effort."

Raef's eyes were wet when he opened them again. He could not force himself to look down, only straight ahead. He shook until he could scarcely keep from falling backward.

"Come."

Raef stepped away from the cliff's edge, then ran to the center of the summit and sat on the cold rock. He hugged himself, shivering.

"I don't trust Zul," Raef said out loud. "I was an Intecessor, a Keeper even, yet I don't trust the Great Spirit."

His own words were a revalation. It shocked him but he knew it was true. He also knew he would have to trust Zul, really trust him, to be free.

Raef slowly stood again, trembling as he did, and walked slowly to the edge of the cliff. He looked down into the swirling mist. Maybe the Spirit would save him. Maybe not. Raef was not sure it mattered any longer.

"I hope you are really there," Raef said.

Then he stepped forward into the void and began to fall.

PART FOUR

FREE FALL

18

Raef was instantly surrounded by mist. His heart leapt to his throat as the white vapor rushed by. He tensed for impact, every muscle clenched. The rush of wind grew stronger as he fell ever faster. Raef gasped for breath.

But there was nothing.

White, all Raef could see was a white void surrounding him. His fingers sliced in vain through the puffs of cold vapor whisking by. The wind tore at his hair and clothes. His lungs jerked irregularly in his chest. He thrashed, uselessly.

I cannot see the ground! He realized, *how long have I left?*

His panic subsided just enough to think. This was too far. He should have hit bottom by now.

Unless…it must be now, I will slam to the rocks now!

His body went rigid again and his sight blurred. Still nothing.

Raef did not want to die. He closed his eyes against the thickening fog and curled into a ball. He had no sense of the sun's location in the sky. His clothing fluttered loudly against the breeze.

Long after he should have hit something, his breathing began to slow. It was quieter now, his hair swirly gently and clothing flapping softly. He was slowing. Which was, he realized, impossible.

He cautiously uncoiled from his fetal position and opened his eyes. Mist swirled slow circles around him. Raef rotated until he faced downward, extending his hands for something to brace against. There was only emptiness. The falling seemed to last forever.

Darkness did come, as it should at sunset, but it came slowly. When it was too dark to see Raef's eyes began to droop.

Where am I? He wondered.

His breathing slowed and his mind drifted to blankness. Raef tried to fight off sleep but he could not keeps his eyes open. In the floating darkness Raef finally fell asleep.

Raef woke with a start. It was light again and the mist around him glowed like snow. He was still falling. His body was rigid and sore. He strained to make sense of what was happening but was unable to. He extended a hand and watched vapor swirl around his fingers. The silence grated at his nerves.

"Zul, are you out there?"

"I am here," came a voice that seemed to emanate from everywhere.

"Am I going to die?"

"No. I have you. You are safe."

"But I am falling!"

"I have you."

"It does not feel like you have me."

"It does not matter what you feel," said Zul's voice, "I have you and you are safe."

All became quiet again. Raef felt panic rise within him.

"Zul?" Raef called, "Zul!"

"Be quiet. Do not talk just now."

"But…"

"Wait. Wait and remain silent. That is all you need do."

Raef closed his mouth, though he yearned to hear Zul's voice again. He waited. The sense of moving downward did not stop, though it was not as strong as before.

It was difficult for Raef to tell how far the sun had journeyed since he woke. It must be nearing mid sun, he reasoned, but the glowing white all around him gave him little bearing. He was not hungry, which struck him as odd.

Raef ebbed and flowed between calm and terror. He tried to relax but his muscles slowly tensed up again. His body ached. It became dark again. He allowed himself to drift from consciousness, not expecting to wake again.

It was the forth time he woke since jumping into the mist when Raef realized he no longer felt like he was falling at all. Mist now swirled slowly around him, coming from all directions. The air was still. He floated in the air, his hair drifting round him in unruly strands. He grew still realizing someone was near.

"You are here again," said Raef.

"I was never gone," said Zul.

"Am I allowed to speak now?"

"Yes."

Raef was silent as he pondered what to say. None of his training as a Keeper prepared him for this. None of the elder Intercessors, none of the sacred scrolls, mentioned anything like this. Raef had never known such singular attention from the Great Spirit. Such scrutiny was as frightening as the falling.

"You want something from me," said Raef.

"That is true."

"I know you wanted me to leave the dragon. I have always known that. But it drew me to itself."

Zul was silent.

"I was never good enough," said Raef, "a failure at all I was asked to do. Rail was the only one who made me feel…acceptable."

"You are acceptable to me," said the voice.

The hair stood up on Raef's neck.

"I…I do not believe you," said Raef. And he knew instantly this was the key to everything.

"I do not believe you want me," Raef continued, "I never did. Even when you appeared to me as a youngling. The village said my vision meant you had chosen me, I wanted to be chosen, but I never really believed any of it."

Raef recalled the rejection by his father of his efforts to impress him. He felt the isolation he experienced from those he had called friends. He remembered running to the dragon as a youngling. He remembered the great beast embracing him.

"You wanted me to come to you," said Raef, "that is what you wanted all along."

"Yes," spoke the voice, "I wanted to ease your

pain."

"I was afraid of you," Raef said, more to himself
than to Zul. It was a revelation. "I was an Intercessor,
afraid of the very spirit I was born to intercede to."

"And why do you fear me?"

"I...I do not believe you. I do not believe you
really want anything to do with me. I was born to the
wrong class, unworthy of my birthright. No, worse
than that, I am a failure at everything. Even here in
Promise, where I am nothing but a common Laborer,
I am an utter disappointment."

"Raef," replied the Great Spirit, "I have pursued
you in spite of what you call failure. And I do not care
what class you are called by. I will call you to
something beyond what you were born to."

A tear escaped Raef's left eye.

"And what of Rail?" said Raef, "I am a dragon
lover. Even after nearly a full season of purging I still
feel its draw on me."

Zul did not respond. Raef pondered his own
words.

"I...I went to Rail. I went to Rail when I should
have come to you."

"I have never given up hope you will come to
me."

Raef tried to imagine going to Zul when he was
sad, alone, rejected. He could not imagine it would
bring comfort. No, to come to the Great Spirit in
such a state would result only in shame.

"I do not trust you," said Raef. "I always said I
trusted you...but I see now that I do not."

"No," said Zul, "you never have."

"Yet to leave Rail I must have someone else to run to. I never understood that before."

"Is there one other than myself who can always be here to meet you?"

"Humans are often distracted," said Raef, "I can only answer, no."

Raef did not hear Zul's voice, but he felt the spirit's confirmation within him. He could not be certain, but it was as if the mist around him was wrapping more closely around him. It was a pleasant thing. Raef was unable to stop a second tear from escaping his eye.

"Zul, I want to trust you. I want to believe you. But I do not know how."

"Be still," came the voice, "stay here with me a while. See what I do, now that you are helpless in my hands."

Silence fell as Raef retold his conversation with Zul in his mind. Dusk began to overtake them.

"You are courageous," said Zul, startling Raef.

"Courageous? In what possible way am I courageous? I have always run from adversity."

"You stepped off a cliff, did you not?"

"I suppose. But I had come to the end of myself. I had little choice."

"Raef, you walked off a cliff many times higher than any man could survive. That is courage, no matter what the reason."

Raef was reluctantly silent.

"And you escaped Black Rock. You were willing to face your home village covered in filth and embarrassed of where you had been."

"No one understood where I had been. They thought I had just gotten lost."

"But you expected them to know where you had been. Willingly living in the dragon's lair for five seasons. You went home, expecting to face what you had done."

"You are making my desperate actions sound like…"

"You left your village rather than put any others at risk," Zul continued, "When you realized you were dangerous, an influence to draw the weak to Rail, you left. You left everything rather than be a potential threat."

"I left out of shame!"

"You left out of the goodness in you. You left because you had the courage to do what was right."

"How can you say I am good?"

"You fought off marauders when they attacked you and Naan on the road. You who have no training with the sword."

"That was luck more than anything."

"I did not intervene to help you," said Zul, "You protected your family on your own."

Raef was silent.

"You are a good man, Raef. You do not believe it yet, but you are a good man."

"I am flawed."

A deep laugh rang out. Raef tingled with confusion.

"Raef, everyone is flawed. Yes, you have flaws, quite a number. But hear me, you are a courageous, loving and good man. That is what I see, when I look upon you."

"Do you really think that of me?"

"I am the Great Spirit. I know that of you."

Raef was silent. The mist was thick around him. Perhaps he could learn to come to Zul rather than Rail. He was not at all sure, but it might be possible.

It grew dark and Raef slept.

When Raef woke he realized he was lying on something solid. He froze at the nearly forgotten sense of being supported by something. He lifted his hand over his face and saw dry fir needles stuck to his skin. He was in the forest.

A hand reached down to him. Raef startled, but the figure standing over him was smiling down. An ancient man with a long white beard and worn robe the color of dust.

"Zul?"

"You dropped something," said the old Spirit, handing a shining blue stone to Raef.

Raef took the stone and smiled weakly.

"Let me help you to your feet," Zul said, "We have a long walk back to Promise."

19

Erif crested a small dune, riding bareback on his black stallion. The horse whinnied loudly and rose up on its hind legs.

"Whoa, there!" cried Erif, "It is only the surf."

The stallion lowered itself but began to prance in a circle, bucking its head. Then Erif saw them. Three dark creatures ran down the beach, directly for him.

"What in all that is sacred are those?"

His stallion bucked again. Erif snatched his long sword from its scabbard and jumped off. The stallion burst away, running back over the dune. The three animals remained focused on Erif.

"Zul, I could use a hand right now," muttered Erif as he raised his sword.

They ran like wolves but had skin like fish. Talons sprung from their paws and fangs hung down below their chins. A thin line of hair ran down their spines to the tips of their whip-like tails. The rest of their bodies were as slick as seals.

"What dark spirit conjured such ugly creatures?" muttered Erif. He swung his sword in a long arch as they approached, catching the muzzle of the first beast. A hiss escaped its maw as it was flung to the side, spraying inky blood over the sand.

A second creature dove at Erif's left calf as he swung the third beast's neck. The sword was too long, catching in the sand before it reached flesh. Unharmed, it backed away and tensed.

"Ah!" cried Erif, as the needled teeth of the second beast pierced his leg, "Cursed beast!"

Erif pulled his sword from the sand and rammed the butt of his grip against the head of the beast biting him. It released him, hissing up at his face. Erif spun away, sweeping his sword in a broad arch.

The third creature turned to the first injured one, now pawing its mangled snout.

Erif swiped at the beast that had bitten him. It got away with only the tip of its tail severed. Erif readied his sword as the three figures hissed and squirmed over the sand.

Lightning exploded from over Erif's right shoulder, striking all three creatures. Erif spun to see Zul standing behind him.

"Get back to Sheeloth from where you came!" shouted the Great Spirit.

"Shee-what?" asked Erif.

The three creatures limped and bounded away, running to the surf and diving beneath the waves.

"What…were those?" asked Erif, bending down to hold the wounds on his leg.

"Neaverling," said Zul, "Minion of Rail."

"One of them injured me badly."

Zul snatched a handful of surf grass and placed it against Erif's wound. The grass glowed blue.

"Ow!" said Erif, "that burns!"

Zul removed his hand and the grass fell away, burned and shriveled. The wound on Erif's leg appeared smaller and bled only a little.

"Their saliva poisons, like that of Rail," said Zul, "only it causes death, not a trance. I have removed the venom."

Erif put his weight on his leg. The pain was mostly gone.

"I have heard nothing of those...neaver... whatever they are. Are they from Black Rock?"

"Their home is called Sheeloth, a place in the east, beyond Black Rock, far past where humans ever go. They live in caves along the coast."

"Why are they here?" asked Erif.

"Rail has sent them," said the spirit, watching the ocean keenly. "I had hoped they would not arrive before you leave this place. It is a long swim from their home. Rail must have sent them when you were first banished."

"But that was three seasons past! They have been swimming since then?"

Zul turned to Erif, "It appears so, and more will come. Rail has many minions." Zul walked over the nearest dune, toward the hills.

Erif followed, limping.

"You see now how much of a threat you are to Rail?" asked Zul. "It has sent its strongest servants to defeat you. It will do all it can to prevent you from returning."

"So much for resting."

"You must be vigilant, my Warrior friend," said
the spirit. "And you should carry your short sword.
These beasts are too small for your long sword to be
much help."

"I have not used the smaller sword since I arrived.
It will need sharpening."

They came to a familiar depression in the ground,
one with a shallow pool within. Zul extended his hand
over the water and it began to stir.

"Let us move forward a few moon cycles in
Raef's story," said Zul, "Raef has entered his twenty
second season. It is the first anniversary of his arrival
in Promise."

Erif peered down into the shapes that were
forming.

--- • ◇ • ---

Raef entered his hut and smiled at Naan.

"Raef, you are filthy and covered in blood," said
his wife.

"The hunt went well!" he replied, "I got a deer
this time, Siro was impressed. We are dressing it
outside."

"Well, if you want me to be impressed, you will
need to change and wash. You smell rank."

Raef bent down and kissed Naan's cheek. She
swatted him playfully away and rolled her eyes.

"Naan, that is a most impressive dress you are
wearing," said Raef, as he removed his soiled tunic. "I
have never seen such beadwork."

"You are not the only one who has learned," she said, "Ura says I am the best illuminator in Promise."

"Illuminator?" asked Raef, "Is not that term reserved for work on parchment?"

"I do not know what else to call it," said Naan, "Illumination is decorating, and I am decorating dresses."

Raef stood back and looked at the intricate beadwork on Naan's dress.

"They wear nothing like this back in Fir Hollow," said Raef.

"We have fewer rituals here," said Naan, "they need something to occupy them, so they decorate everything," said Naan. "I kind of like it."

Raef washed himself by the corner basin, behind a privacy curtain, and dressed in his nicest tunic and trousers. He came out and hugged Naan from behind as she stirred the kettle of pottage.

"We have come a long way, have we not?" he asked.

"Perhaps," said Naan, "though I cannot be sure you have really changed."

Raef stepped back from his wife, "Not changed? What is that supposed to mean? I am an entirely different man! I can hunt, we have plenty of food, I have not even thought of the dragon or Black Rock in many moon cycles!"

"So you say," said Naan, "and I supposed I am simply supposed to believe you."

"Naan, what are you saying?"

"Raef, you have been gone for four suns. When you used to go away like that, it meant you were visiting that…that dragon."

"Naan, I was with Siro, Ian, Jesson and Ramey. I was never alone."

Naan huffed, and then spooned pottage into bowls on the table.

Raef took the meat that had been roasting over the fire and placed it on a wooden plank on the table. He removed the cover on the saltcellar and helped Nine up onto the bench, next to him.

"Raef, what are you doing with Nine?"

"She is old enough to have a bit of solid food."

Naan sat opposite Raef, shaking her head slowly.

Raef eyed his wife, wishing he knew how to assure her. He knew he was different, since stepping off the mountain. He could not understand why Naan could not see it also.

After last meal Raef asked Naan to come sit by the fire pit outside with the others. It was a warm summer night and the stars were in clear view.

Naan sat across the fire from Raef, with some of the other women. Raef started to follow her, but decided it best to stay with the men. Nine sat on his lap, apparently excited to see him after four suns away.

"I am beginning to like it here in Promise," said Raef.

"You are definitely doing well," said Jesson. "I had only fifteen seasons when I was rescued from Black Rock, but it took me five seasons after arriving here to stop looking for Rail."

"It was not that many moon cycles ago when I last failed," Raef replied.

"One who has been a Dragon Child cannot

expect to never feel the pull of the dragon," said Jesson, "but you are doing better than I. This is only your first season."

Raef followed Naan to the hut when he saw her return. She took Nine from him, changed her, and put her on the small straw mattress they had made for her.

Raef changed into his sleeping robe and got into bed with Naan. The window was open and he could see the moon.

"It is good we came here," he said, "You were right to want to seek out Tup."

Naan did not respond.

"Naan, I love you so much. I have always loved you, but since coming her I feel...so much more."

He waited for her to respond, but Naan remained silent.

"Naan?"

"What, Raef?"

"Do you...do you love me?"

There was silence, then the sound of soft crying.

"Raef, it is still too soon. It is not fair to ask me that yet."

20

Raef returned from the crop field at mid sun, entering the circle of huts that was Promise.

"Have you seen Tren?" Raef asked Siro. "He has not been in the fields for more suns than I can count."

Siro stood up from a short log he and Jesson had been sawing.

"Do not fret, young friend," said Ian. "Tren has been carving another of his bowls."

"Ah," said Raef, looking back at the women and greenling following him from the field. "Tren does work with stone like no one I have seen."

Raef turned back to the men, who were sawing a log into long boards. He admired how slim the men had managed to make the slices.

"You two cut so evenly," Raef remarked, "The craftsmen in Fir Hollow could not match this."

"This is only the beginning," said Jesson, "Siro is the finest woodworker in Promise."

"I know," said Raef, "I have seen the furniture in his hut. I only wish I could do something like that."

"Join us for purging?" asked Jesson.

After purging Raef returned to his hut for the mid sun meal. Naan was inside working: three flowery dresses lay over the table.

"Oh, sorry, husband," she said, "I was working and have not cleared the table."

"No need to move them," said Raef, picking up one dress. The beadwork sparkled. "We can sit by the window to eat."

"I wonder why no one uses bowls for potage in Fir Hollow," said Naan, spooning meaty pottage into three of Tren's creations. "It makes it so much easier to take the food anywhere to eat."

After the meal Raef left the hut and walked across the circle to Ian's hut. The community elder was around back, stringing a bow.

"Ian, my old friend, can I join you on a hunt in the next few suns?" asked Raef.

"Thank you for the offer, Raef, but a few of us are taking Bolin's oldest son on his first hunt," Ian replied, "Besides, we have done so well on the last hunt there is already plenty left over for you and Naan. You do not even need to come!"

Raef turned and walked back to his hut, which sat on the edge of the field. Women and young greenlia were already picking up hoes and walking down the rows to start work again.

"Zul," said Raef, "are you here?"

"I am here," came a voice behind Raef.

Raef turned, startled to see the ancient spirit standing behind him, in solid form.

"Zul, I did not really expect…"

"To see me?"

"Well, yes."

"What is it?" asked the spirit.

"I just feel…so useless here."

The spirit grinned.

"So…worthless," continued Raef. "No on values me here. No one needs an Intercessor in a village where the spirits appear to anyone who wishes to speak to them."

"What does that have to do with your value?" asked Zul.

"I have nothing to offer."

"Raef, I am here, right now, talking to you, because I value you," said Zul, "just like you are."

"I…I do not feel valued. I suppose I need to learn to feel it."

"No," said Zul, "not yet. Just try to believe it. Feelings come later. Right now, you cannot trust your feelings. They are still too polluted by the essence of Rail."

Raef tried to smile.

Zul faded from sight.

Raef picked up his hoe and walked to the garden to start weeding.

21

Erif recorded the last scene he had watched, and then carefully wrapped up his writing quill. The quill was new, and as birds were hard to catch he wanted it to last. He dabbed a finger on the ink, testing it to see that it was dry, then rolled up the parchment. After stowing the scroll in a wooden chest Erif picked up the shorter of his swords.

"This will need sharpening," he said, "but that can wait until dark."

He mounted his stallion and rode to the beach, then got off and removed its reigns.

"Go, run for a while!" said Erif, slapping the stallion's side. He watched the powerful beast charge down the strip of sand.

"Such power," he mumbled.

Erif swept the sword through the air. *It feels so light,* he thought. *I suppose it would after using the longer sword for so many seasons.*

He practiced charging and retreating, the sword

flashing in the sun. *This will take a while to grow accustomed to again.*

"Do not worry."

Erif stopped and turned to see Zul standing on the sand nearby.

"Zul, you are here."

"I have been watching you," said the spirit.

"You are always watching me," said Erif.

"Yes, and you can stop training now."

"But, the Neaverling."

"I have seen where they are. The three you fought are waiting to heal before attacking again. The others are still out at sea. You are safe for a bit longer. It is more important that you heal before you train."

"As you wish," said Erif, "it just feels like I should be doing something."

"Ah," said Zul, "like Raef you fear you have no value without doing something impressive."

"No, no..." said Erif. "Well, maybe a little. Just sometimes."

The Great Spirit smiled.

Raef stood next to Tup on the mountain summit. Before them was a small pool of water left after a rain.

"What are we waiting for?" asked Raef.

"For Zul."

"Zul?" asked Raef, "But you are a wizard."

Tup smiled in reply.

A form began to appear next to Tup, one that Raef immediately recognized as the Great Spirit. Tup extended his staff to Zul. The spirit took hold of the top of the staff with his fingers. The cracks in the staff began to glow with blue light. The light became more intense, slowly washing over the entire staff.

"The power comes from Zul?" asked Raef.

"Of course," replied Tup, "did you think I was a dark wizard?"

"But I was taught…" Raef began.

"That wizards are evil?" asked Zul, still holding the end of Tup's staff. "The Keepers taught you that."

"Yes," said Raef.

"Tell me, Raef," asked Zul, "did you ever see one of those Keepers show any sign of my power?"

"Well…not really."

"Did you ever see me appear to any of them?"

"No," answered Raef, "they said they sometimes saw visions of you."

"Because they were not close to me, not like Tup," said Zul.

"But…they were Keepers!" said Raef.

"What is that to me?" asked Zul. "You are an outcast and I am appearing to you. What does that tell you?"

Before Raef could answer, Zul released the glowing staff and faded from sight.

Raef looked down on Tup, who smiled softly back.

"Shall we begin?" asked the wizard.

Tup waved his staff over the pool of water. The water began to ripple and become cloudy.

Raef peered into the water, seeing an image take shape as the water cleared and grew still. A small youngling sat on the floor of a hut, playing with a toy wooden horse.

"Do you recognize him?" asked Tup.

"That…looks like me," said Raef.

"When you were quite small. You look happy."

Tup moved his staff over the water and it rippled, changing the image within it.

"How do you do that?" asked Raef.

"I do not," replied Tup. "Now tell me what you see."

"It is me once again, but I am nearly a greenling." Raef looked at the image of himself. He was in a large lodge, the Community Lodge, surrounded by others. Most were younglings, like him. He recognized his old friends, Domik, an Intercessor, and Chaz, the son of a Warrior. Adults stood off at the sides, talking and laughing together.

"What is happening?" asked Tup, "Why are all these people around you?"

"This is the celebration of my twelfth season," said Raef. "It was in the Common Lodge, because my father had influence in the village."

"Influence?"

"Yes, only Nobles have private celebrations in the Common Lodge. But my father arranged for my celebration to be held there."

"Hm, then that makes it all the more odd," said Tup.

"What?"

"Look at your face, Raef. What do you see?"

"I see nothing unusual."

"Are you certain? This is your celebration, the last

before Youngling's End. No small event. Your friends are all around you. You have the privilege of celebrating in the Common Lodge. So...why is it you are not smiling?"

Raef peered closer. It was true; the image of him did not smile. In fact, he saw emptiness in his young eyes. He looked almost sad.

"Even at only twelve seasons, Rail had taken much away from you," said Tup.

"I was in the forest with the dragon every sun," said Raef. "I was obsessed with it."

"As you have been since," said Tup.

"Why are you showing me this?"

"So you would see for yourself and believe. You have lived most of your seasons unable to see what is really happening around you. Unable to feel joy. Now, that limitation is being removed."

"I still do not feel joy," said Raef.

"Not yet," said the wizard, "but your mind is clear. All the energy you spent imagining yourself with Rail is now free to be used in other ways."

"I do not follow your meaning," said Raef.

"You will find that you have a new ability to think clearly and creatively," said Tup, "you will have more energy to work with. You will discover things you excel at that you never imagined before."

"That is absurd," said Raef, "I am nothing more than a common Laborer now. I have no skills. I have been lucky a few times hunting, but other than that I am of little use to anyone."

Tup's smile grew wider.

"How can you possibly know such things?" asked

Raef, "Do you claim to see the future?"

Tup raised his staff, which began to glow brightly, "I am a wizard, after all. You know how little we can be trusted."

Raef felt himself blush. He looked down into the pool, at the sad image of himself. The image faded.

Do I dare hope that Tup is right?

22

Raef's back stung as he bent over in the sun, frozen snow hitting between the spots sizzling essence in a painful mix. He wanted it to force the memory of sunset past from his mind, but it did not.

He had meant it as a playful joke when he stuck his foot out to trip Ian's youngest son as he ran past him. But the youngling had fallen into the fire pit and burned his arm rather badly. Raef shook his head, but the memory replayed again.

Tren's voice brought him back to the present. Only Ramey and Tren were with him, the others out on a long hunt.

"Nothing like a little snow to make the purging even more unbearable," said Tren.

"It is not so bad," said Ramey, who began to pull his under shirt on.

"That is easy for you to say," said Raef, grabbing his own tunic, "your back is scarcely scarred and I never see essence leaking out you when you purge."

"Raef is right, Ramey," teased Tren, "You do not have to endure what we do."

"You have only yourself to blame for that, Tren" said Ramey; "Your back would be healed by now if you did not keep sneaking off to find the dragon."

"You went out again?" asked Raef, turning to Tren.

Tren's smile vanished and he hung his head, "Sunrise past, I went out in the forest alone, looking for it."

"I apologize if my question is rude," said Raef, "but why do you keep going after the dragon when you have been here so long? How many seasons have you lived here in Promise?"

Tren did not answer.

At least I did not go looking for Rail again, though Raef.

"Tren and I arrived in Promise ten seasons past," said Ramey, "We were rescued by Tup, along with Jesson and a few others."

"Ten seasons," said Raef, "that means you left Black Rock when you had only twelve seasons, still a youngling."

"That is correct," said Ramey, "And I had been at Black Rock for less that two full seasons. That is why I have so few scars."

"I had fourteen seasons when Tup rescued us," said Tren, "But I had been at Black Rock for several seasons already."

The three men vested their tunics and coats, and then walked back to the huts.

The memory of Ian's son falling into the fire returned to Raef. The other men became oddly silent as they walked.

"Why do you not return to one of the villages?" Raef asked Ramey, attempting to break the silence. "With so little essence and so many seasons to heal, could you not just leave now?"

"I have been here since a youngling," Ramey replied. "This is all I know. I can scarcely recall what living in a village is like."

"I need to be here a few more seasons," said Raef, "but I cannot imagine living here forever. It seams so…isolated."

Ramey shrugged and smiled. Tren did not speak. Tren walked on to his hut in silence. Raef and Ramey stopped outside Raef's hut.

"You were right to question Tren about seeking out Rail," said Ramey. "Someone needs to make him think. I worry about him."

Raef paused, waiting to see if Ramey would comment on the accident with Ian's son. He did not.

Raef stood in the snow and watched Ramey return to his hut. No one else was outside. Smoke drifted from the roof of each hut and the smell of food was in the air. Raef tried me make himself enter his hut, but he found he could not.

"Zul…what have I done?" Raef asked the sky.

"You have been human," came Zul's voice from behind.

Raef spun to see the old spirit, dressed in his usual tattered robe.

"Are you not cold without a coat?" asked Raef.

"That is your concern?" asked Zul. "Suddenly you are not worried about yourself?"

Raef hung his head, "I do not know what to

think of anything. I am just...confused...afraid... sorry I hurt my friend's son."

"Ah, the fire," said Zul.

Raef felt a tear on his cheek.

"I am still a danger to everyone," said Raef, "even after leaving the dragon."

"You made a mistake," said Zul, "that does not make you dangerous."

"I feel so bad."

"I know," said Zul. "I am happy you called for me."

"I wish you could make the hurt go away."

"That would be nice," said Zul, "but it is better that you learn not to fear it."

"Fear what?"

"Fear difficult feelings," said the spirit, "You must learn that they will not destroy you. You do not have to run from them."

"So, what am I do to?"

"What you have just done," said Zul, "call me and talk."

"Oh. Yes, I suppose I did call you."

"And that makes me happier than you can imagine," said the Great Spirit. "Would you like to invite me in to share a meal with you and Naan?"

"You would do that?" asked Raef.

"Yes, I would."

23

Erif finished reading the letter from Tama, his eyes wet with tears. He looked up to see the prison barge that had brought it sail out of sight.

"This is not fair," said Erif. "It should not be so hard for her. She did nothing wrong."

"No, it is not fair," said Zul.

"She has run out of money," said Erif, "She sold the last of our belongings, other than clothes, but she said the food would run out by the end of the moon cycle. By now that has passed, since she wrote this letter."

"She is strong, Erif," said Zul, "She and your younglings will survive."

Erif sunk to his knees and cried.

Zul knelt beside him.

"I am watching over them as well," said Zul, "I will not allow serious harm to come to them."

"But they still suffer."

"As do you," said Zul, "Each of you has a

journey to make before you are reunited."

"I cannot even send her a message to encourage her," said Erif, "I cannot even finish her letters before the boat leaves."

"But you had written a letter, one that the boat is taking to her," said Zul.

"I did not know about this," said Erif, "I would have written more encouragement."

Zul put his hand on Erif's shoulder.

"She knows you care," said Zul, "She knows."

"I suppose it is time to see more of Raef's journey," said Erif.

"Yes," said Zul, "when you are ready."

"I am ready now."

Raef followed Zul to a tide pool. He watched the water ripple and Raef appear. The young man walked down a dusty path, kicking at the dirt.

"I have moved us forward, a bit more than a season," said Zul. "Raef is approaching his twenty fourth seasons. It is spring."

Raef bent over and fingered a limp plant. He stood up and wrapped his coat tighter around himself. He heard a noise and turned to see Evot and Siro enter the crop field, walking toward him.

"How does it look, Raef?" asked Evot.

"Worse than before," said Raef, "most of the crops are wilting."

The two older men came to stand by Raef, looking down at the sad row of plants.

"I thought water was to be brought from the

stream," said Siro.

"It was," said Raef, "but the stream is nearly dry. It was so shallow we could scarcely get any water in the buckets. We worked all day to little success."

Evot bent down and pulled at a limp leaf.

"If these die we will have to replant," Evot said, "We will be lucky to get much of a crop at all."

"Has this happened before?" asked Raef.

"Not this bad," said Siro. "We rarely have drought here, and when we do it has always been in summer."

"But this spring there was almost no rain," said Evot.

"And not much snow in winter," said Raef, "At least compared to the first two winters Naan and I have been here."

"I cannot remember a winter with so little snow," said Evot. "Now there is none left to melt and fill the stream."

"What are we going to do?" asked Raef.

"I do not know," said Siro, "Perhaps the rain will begin. The crops are not a total loss yet."

Raef followed the men to the huts. He waited for one of them to offer encouragement. Neither did. Raef returned to his hut.

Naan was kneading bread dough on the table. Nine ran to him, hugging his legs.

"Daddy!"

"Hello, little one," he said, picking her up.

"Why are you home so soon?" asked Naan.

"There is nothing to do in the fields," said Raef, "not even the weeds can grow."

Naan turned and wiped her hands on her apron.

"Should I be worried?" she asked.

"Raef put Nine on his shoulders, feeling her small hands grip his hair. She giggled.

"I am beginning to worry," said Raef. "Evot and Siro said Promise has never had so little water. And it is only spring. If it does not rain soon, and rain a lot, we may loose the entire crop."

"The dried vegetables from last year will last until mid summer," said Naan, "but after that, I do not know what we would eat."

"Perhaps we could search the forest for plants to eat," said Raef.

"The forest has no more rain than our field," said Naan. "Why would we expect to find food there?"

"I fear you are right," said Raef. "That means the animals will go hungry too, affecting hunting, I would imagine."

"Daddy, we go outside?" said Nine.

"Take her," said Naan, "It will give you something to do."

Raef took Nine outside and walked in a circle around the smoldering fire pit. A few other younglings played around him, but most were still inside. The summer sun had not come to warm the air.

"I see you have as little work as I," said Jesson, coming from his hut.

"Other than fret about the crops," said Raef.

"Take advantage of this," said Jesson, "Spend some time with Nine."

Five younglings burst from Jesson's hut, the smallest just able to walk. They clung to their father like mice, trying to climb his legs.

"I see you have your hands full," said Raef.

Jesson laughed, lifting his eldest into the air.

Raef took Nine off his shoulders and put her on the ground. He held her hand and took her through the field, beyond the barns, past the meadow where the men purged, and to the stream at the edge of the trees.

"Look, water, Daddy!" said Nine.

"Well, not much," said Raef.

Nine walked into the mud, stamping her little feet until her new leather shoes were covered in muck.

"Your mother will scold us both," said Raef.

He picked her up and tossed her into the air. Her hair was blond and already quite long. Raef watched his daughters golden hair sparkle in the sun.

"More, more, Daddy!"

When the sun reached mid sky, Raef returned Nine to her mother, after carefully cleaning her shoes first. He joined the men for purging then returned to his hut for mid sun meal. Nine napped after eating and Raef rested with a mug of ale.

"What now?" asked Naan.

"I do not know," said Raef, trying to hide his agitation, "There is not even a hunt planned for several more suns."

"Then just rest, husband," she said, leaning back in her seat and closing her eyes.

Raef closed his eyes as well, and an old familiar pull came to his chest. For an instant he saw the face of Rail.

"I think I will go find Zul," said Raef, standing

up, "or maybe Jesson."

"You are not going to rest?" asked Naan.

"Not now," he said, "I think I need to get out of the hut."

Naan grew a puzzled look on her face, then shrugged and closed her eyes again.

Raef went outside to find someone to talk with.

PART FIVE

PROMISE REVEALED

24

"Congratulations!" said Ian, slapping Raef on the shoulder. "You have survived twenty four seasons!"

Raef smiled as cheers went up, along with mugs of ale. He scooted a bit farther away from the bonfire, as the night was already warm.

"I am still unaccustomed to celebrating the seasons in ones life," said Raef, still smiling. "In the villages, we stop such things after Youngling's End."

"I like celebratings!" said Nine, spinning in circles in front of Raef.

Raef smiled at his daughter. Her hair is nearly as long as mine, he thought. How the seasons have flown by.

"I am going to have to stop calling you 'young man,'" laughed Ian, "you and Ramey have surpassed your youth."

"I think it is time for someone else to take that calling," said Raef, pointing to a tall greenling sitting next to Evot. "Evot, does not your son reach seventeen seasons soon?"

"Indeed he does!" said Evot, slapping his son's

back. "And he had better pick a wife."

The greenling blushed and looked away.

Naan came and sat on Raef's lap, one arm around his neck, the other holding a mug of ale.

"Almost three seasons we have been here," Naan said, kissing Raef, "Congratulations indeed, my husband."

The celebrating continued well into the moon. Raef and Naan were among the last to retire to their hut, carrying a sleeping Nine with them as they did.

"I like how they celebrate anniversaries here," said Naan.

"I suppose it makes up for all the other ceremonies they ignore," said Raef.

"Stop it," said Naan; slapping his arm, "I know you enjoyed this."

"I will admit it, if I must," he said, crawling into bed.

Raef slept easily. His dreams no longer interrupted with visions of dragons or Black Rock. Even the worry of the drought drifted away. At least until next sunrise.

"I had better go inspect the crops," he said, after first meal. "I have put off looking for long enough."

"Try not to become too sad," said Naan, "not so soon after your celebration."

Raef smiled at this wife, tussled his daughter's hair, and went outside to find the other men.

Ian, Siro and Evot were sitting around the still smoldering fire pit. Evot's eldest son was with them.

"Shall we inspect the crops?" asked Raef.

Ian gave a long sigh. "I am afraid of what I will

see," said the elder, "as we have had no rain for a full moon cycle."

Raef walked with the men and Evot's son to the fields. Raef noted the dust wafting in the air above the crops as they approached. They stopped when they came to the center of the field.

"Only a third of the crops have survived," said Siro, "and the survivors are quite stunted."

"This is not enough," said Ian, waving his arms in a circle, "not enough for us to survive winter."

"Well, not for all of us to survive," said Raef, "I suppose some of us could move elsewhere."

The men looked at Raef with shocked faces.

"I am joking!" said Raef.

Ian looked up at Raef and chuckled, "You are not the man who came to us three seasons back."

"No," said Siro, "you have indeed changed."

"For the better, I hope," said Raef. "So, what do we do about the crops?"

"I do not know," said Ian. "I truly do not know."

Raef paused as the other four began to walk toward the huts. They did not stop, so he dashed after them.

"You are not going to do anything?" asked Raef.

"What can we do?" asked Evot.

"I do not know, but we cannot just wait until the food runs out."

Siro reached up and patted Raef's shoulder. Everyone but Raef walked to his hut. Raef stood, stunned, in the center of the circle of huts. He loosened the strings at the front of his tunic and sat on a stump near the fire pit.

I am not giving up, he thought. *There must be another way.*

Ura, Ian's wife, and Iris, Siro's wife, came outside, each carrying several dresses. The beadwork down the fronts of the garments sparkled in the sun.

Ian's daughters followed the women, carrying a table. The table was placed on the ground and the women lay the dresses on it and began to stitch more beads.

Raef head turned at the sound of repeated sharp cracks coming from Tren's hut. *More bowls,* thought Raef, *as if he did not already have more than all of Promise will ever use.*

Laughing from behind him caused Raef to turn again, this time to see Jesson and a greenling carrying an ornately carved table from one of the barns.

"Is it finished?" Raef shouted.

"Come look!" Jesson returned.

Raef stood, walking to meet them at the edge of the field. The table was oiled to a dark, glossy finish. A strip down the center ornately carved, the sides gently scalloped, curved legs ending in carved paws completed the piece.

"This is amazing," he said.

"Siro is quite good," said Jesson, "but I am learning. I did the finishing this time."

"I have it!" said Raef, slapping the tabletop. "I know what to do!"

Raef ran to Ian's hut and called loudly, "Ian, Ian, come out!"

The door opened and the older man peeked out.

"What is it, my energetic friend?"

"I know what we can do!"

"About what?" asked Ian.

"About the crops!"

Ian's face remained passive, other than lifted eyebrows.

"Listen," said Raef, "you people, almost everyone in Promise, you can all do amazing things with wood and stone and beads. When Naan and I went to Midland, I saw nothing like what you do in all the market stalls there. Midland is the largest market in all of the Great Province, and there was nothing to compare to what you do here!"

"That is nice, Raef," said Ian, "but that does not bring more rain."

"It does not need to!" said Raef. He stepped back and gazed up at the sky, peering off in each direction.

"Surely the weather is not the same in all of the Great Province," Raef continued. "Certainly not every village is experiencing drought."

Ian squinted at Raef, "What are you trying to say?"

Raef grasped the older man's hands. "Ian, we can sell these things! They would fetch a very good price, especially in Midland. We could use the money to buy food. It matters not if we get rain or not this season."

"Sell?" said Ian, "Raef, that would mean leaving Promise."

"Of course!" said Raef, "It is a brilliant idea!" He took a few steps toward the women, who had stopped working and were gazing at Raef, "No one has heard of this place. We can offer mysterious merchandise from an unknown village. I can see it now, Ian. In a city like Midland they would be fighting over your wares."

"Raef," said Ian, "why would anyone want to buy these things? They are just bowls, and tables and garments."

"No they are not! I have never seen anyone decorate objects like you do here. No one puts this much effort into common objects. No one has the occasion. Every where else there is too much work to be done."

"That is why we stay here," replied Ian, "we do not want to live as the others do—so many rituals to follow, taxes to pay, Nobles and Warriors to support."

"We can live here," said Raef, "but nothing stops us from selling elsewhere."

"Raef, why would someone spend much needed money for objects that serve no better than what they already own?" asked Ian, "who could even afford that?"

"You have been in Promise too long," said Raef, "Not everyone in the Province is poor. There are enough Nobles and wealthy Merchants to buy all we could ever produce. And the likes of them want items like these. To impress."

Ian's face turned sour, "We do not make these to impress! We make them out of the enjoyment of the craft."

"Then you would not mind selling them?" asked Raef.

Ian put his palm to his forehead, "Raef, if you want to try to sell some of these things, you may. But I am too old for such nonsense. Perhaps some of the younger ones would help you."

"I can convince them," said Raef. "Of course, we will have to build another wagon or two to carry everything. And everyone would need to make as many pieces as they could before the trip. We would probably need two or three moon cycles to prepare."

"Fine, fine," said Ian, "but allow the men to keep hunting when they need to. We still need meat."

"Of course, Ian," said Raef. "Do not worry, I think this will work."

25

"Go back where you came from!" shouted Erif, bringing his sword down on the neck of the nearest Neaverling.

Dark blood soaked the sand as the beast dropped to the ground. Two others in front of Erif took several steps back.

They had surrounded him in his camp, five in all, plus the one with a mangled snout who kept its distance, still too injured to fight. Erif's back was to a short earthen wall, dotted with caves where he kept his belongings.

A small Neaverling crept around Erif to his right, keeping a fair distance, then charging for something behind Erif.

"Do not try sneaking around me," said Erif, spinning and swiping his sword to sever the tip of a Neaverling's tail.

It darted away with a whelp.

"What were you after?" Erif muttered, "you were

not charging me."

He spun back to face the four that were left blocking his escape route. Erif looked back and forth between the caves and the creatures.

"You are after the scrolls," he said. "How did you even know they exist, much less where I hid them?"

One of the creatures hissed and curled its black lips at Erif.

"Are you smiling?" asked Erif, "You are not mere beasts, are you? You are spirits!"

One Neaverling licked its newly shortened tail but the remaining three lunged in unison, two at Erif and one to get around him on the left.

Erif jumped at the creature to his left, just as it was passing him, impaling it between its shoulder blades with his sword. Ripping the sword back, he spun in the air, dodging the other two as they passed under him. The impaled Neaverling stumbled to the ground as Erif brought his sword down on another's back.

"I am a Warrior!" shouted Erif, raising his sword against the remaining uninjured beast, "Unlike the Warriors back in the Province, I know how to fight spirits like you."

The creature opened its needle-toothed mouth and hissed loudly as the short-tailed Neaverling made a charge.

Erif ran backward; blocking the entrance to the caves, then lowered his sword to the charging best. It stopped and hissed, talons digging into the sand.

"There are only two of you left," said Erif, "you will not defeat me. You will not take the scrolls."

"Nooo Warrior," hissed the uninjured creature.

"You speak!" said Erif. "I should not be surprised."

"You are only a Prissssoner," hissed the second, "not a Warrior."

Erif grinned, "That will not work on me. I know Rail's tricks. And I do know who I am."

The Neaverling with the severed tail began to quiver, its muscular legs rippling.

"We wait for the otherssss," said the uninjured Neaverling. "Together, we will defeat you."

Erif remained poised to strike as the two creatures carried the dead away. Those that could crept after them.

How many will come? Erif wondered. *I was scarcely able to fight off these five; I do not know that I could do it again, much less fight off more.*

———.✦.———

Raef pounded a nail to secure a plank to the side of the newest wagon. He looked to his sides, watching the two greenlings assisting him secure the last planks, completing the wagon. They were Evot's suns, both approaching adulthood.

"Well done," said Raef.

"Thank you," said the eldest, "but I do not know if we can assist you much more. Our father says we are neglecting our other duties."

"This is our best chance to survive the winter," said Raef. "Do not worry, your father will see."

"It is not only our father," said the younger, "All of the elders are opposed to your idea. They say we cannot afford to expend so much energy on such a futile plan."

"There is only one more wagon to build," said Raef, "But I can find others if you two cannot help again."

"We like your idea," said the eldest brother, "We will help again if we are able."

"That is all I can ask," said Raef.

They returned to the huts where Raef waited for the men to join him for purging. Siro and Jesson came to meet him.

"Shall we go?" asked Siro.

"Where are the others?" asked Raef.

"They are not coming," said Jesson.

"Not coming?" asked Raef, "But we must purge."

Siro shrugged and began walking to the barns. Jesson followed. Raef waited for an explanation, but none was given.

Raef returned home for the mid sun meal after purging. Nine was waiting inside and ran to meet him. Raef scooped her up and tossed her in the air. Nine squealed with glee.

"You forget how tall you are," said Naan. "You will toss her up through the roof if you are not careful."

"I would never hurt Nine!" laughed Raef, nuzzling his daughter, nose to nose.

Naan grinned and swatted Raef on the behind.

Raef sat at the table, Nine by his side. Nine lifted a spoonful of pottage to her mouth, spilling half onto the table.

"How is the construction proceeding?" asked

Naan.

"We finished the second wagon," said Raef, "only one more to build."

"Do you think we need that many?" she asked, "we still have our little cart."

"Yes, but that will be for our own food and tents to sleep in. Tren and some others are making as much as they can to sell. I want to have enough room to fit everything."

Naan grew silent, looking down into her bowl as she ate.

"What it is?" asked Raef.

"I am confused by this place," said Naan, "When we first arrived, everyone was so supportive and kind. But it has not been the same the last moon cycle."

"What do you mean?"

"Ura has been helping me make clothing to sell," said Naan, "and she says Ian has been quite cross with her about helping us."

"That is surprising," said Raef. "Ian is normally so gracious."

"And I have heard that Siro has been acting quite unreasonably," Naan continued, "Ira complains that he has been treating her inconsiderately for some suns."

"Well," said Raef, "to be fair, we are all under quite a bit of stress, with the crops failing and still no rain."

"But Raef, even so, Promise is a place of healing. I would think these people would be beyond such pettiness by now."

Raef patted his daughters back, who smiled up at

him.

"Ian, Evot, Tren and Ramey did not come to purging," said Raef. "Tren does not surprise me, but the others do. Neglecting purging is serious. I do not understand why they would behave this way."

"Perhaps they simply tried to impress us when we were new," said Naan. "Perhaps this is how they lived before we arrived."

"I do not wish to speculate," said Raef. "I only hope this does not last."

26

Squalls of rain pelted the rocks as Erif crept down the slick rocks. His long sword, which he had been training with before the storm, was strapped to his back. Nearly as long as he, it made climbing difficult. His foot slipped and he slid sideways in the wind. His sword came untied and clattered to the rocks below. His feet slid out from under him and he slid down a steep boulder on his stomach, scratching for purchase with his fingers. He finally found a crevice to grip, his legs dangling in the air above a dangerously high drop.

How am I going to get off this rock? He thought.

The wind blew his body sideways. Erif gathered his strength and lifted himself up with his arms, lifting a knee to pull his body back onto the boulder. He rolled to his back and panted.

The rain increased to a torrential downpour, the wind to a gale. Erif turned to his stomach and crawled along the ridge of rock until he came to the place it met sand. He started to search for his sword, but decided to run for camp instead.

This is not a storm of nature, he realized, *there is evil behind this.*

The clouds darkened, boiling downward over the island. Erif was blown into a shrub by a blast of wind. He staggered back to the trail and ran.

Where is Zul when I actually need him?

He came to his camp to find it nearly destroyed. The hillside where he had dug the caves had liquefied and washed down to cover his camp. His eating table stuck up through the mud, smashed to bits.

"The scrolls!" shouted Erif.

He ran up onto the mound of mud and dug down over the spot he believed had once been the cave where he kept his box of scrolls. Sandy earth continued to flow down, filling the hole as fast as Erif dug.

Erif stood, ankle deep in muck, and yelled at the clouds, "You think you can stop me? You think I will give up?"

A flash, so bright it nearly blinded Erif, erupted in the clouds. Slivers of lightning instantly surrounded Erif as thunder deafened him. Erif stood, stunned, ears ringing, trying to make sense of the spherical shape the lacy bolts had formed around him.

"Enough!" shouted a deep voice.

Erif turned to see Zul nearby, waving his arms wide. The clouds flew upward, parting to reveal a blue sky.

Erif shivering. The rain stopped.

"Was that Rail?" asked Erif.

"I am afraid so," said Zul.

"I did not know…I did not realize…"

"That it was so powerful?" asked Zul. "You have not yet learned all its secrets," said Zul.

The Great Spirit walked to Erif, took his arm, and led him to a rock.

Erif sat, trembling.

"It only expends such energy in the most desperate situations," said Zul. "The dragon will require a full moon cycle to recover."

"Unfortunately," Erif stammered, "I am out here, banished on this island, and cannot strike Rail in its weakened state."

"What is more urgent," said Zul, "is for you to find the scrolls. They may be damaged."

"Why are the scrolls so important?" asked Erif.

"So the Province will know the truth about Rail."

"I still have difficulty believing anyone will take them seriously."

"That will be up to each who reads them," said Zul, "But it is only fair that we warn them."

——•◇•——

"I do not understand," said Raef, "most of them were not at Black Rock nearly as long as I was. They carry fewer scars."

Tup smiled at him, sitting on a round stone across from Raef. The air was dry, a slight breeze wafting across the mountain summit.

"The others," Raef continued, "those who you rescued from Black Rock, should they not be farther along by now? I have only been here three seasons, but I have not even considered the dragon for nearly a full season. Tren continues to seek it out. And now I am seeing that even some of the elders are neglecting the purging. I fear for them. Am I deluded?"

"No, you are not deluded, Raef," said the small wizard, "You are healing well. In spite of all your scars, you have progressed beyond most of the others."

"But why? What is so special about me?"

"Do not misunderstand," said Tup, "you still have much to learn and will still make mistakes in the future. But you are what you have become because of one simple fact. When you realize there is something you need to do, no matter how much you may not want to, you see it through."

"But, I have done nothing special."

"Raef," said Tup, leaning forward, "it is not always the grand things that make the difference. It is often many small things, strung together."

Raef shrugged, "I do not feel I have been particularly steadfast."

"You still cannot see, can you?" asked the Wizard, "Where is that stone I gave you?"

Raef pulled a leather pouch from his waist tie and handed it to the Wizard.

Tup removed the blue stone and admired it.

"Raef, you have the courage of many men. You are not the meek youngling you remember yourself as. You are the Intercessor willing to submit to healing even if it takes him to an old Wizard. You are the brave man who continues to endure purging even when others do not. You are resolute husband and father who takes on even the most menial task to feed his family."

Raef looked at the ground. He startled at the touch of Tup's hand on his chin, lifting his head to see eye to eye.

"A man," said Tup, "who will walk off a cliff, if that is what it takes."

27

Erif pried the lid of the wooden box open and peered inside. Mud and sand surrounded the scrolls.

"These are all ruined!" he said.

"Do not assume," said the old spirit. "Check each one."

Erif pulled one scroll out, untying it and opening it to the sun.

"The edges are damp," said Erif, "but the ink has not been wet. I think it will be saved if I unroll it to dry in the sun."

"Good," said Zul, "we should probably take each out to dry."

Erif took the scroll to a high point above his camp, unrolling it to its full span, which was nearly twice as long as Erif was tall. He used stones at the corners and edges to hold it down.

"I will remain here," said Zul, "to keep the beasts away."

Erif returned to his camp and pulled three more

scrolls out. One was particularly soggy. *It is bad enough that I have to stay out here alone,* he thought, *but having to write all these scrolls, and now having to protect them from strange spirits is more than I deserve.* He carried them to Zul and began unrolling each.

"It appears this one is beyond saving," said Erif, "I believe I can still read it, for the most part, but the parchment is so wet it is falling apart."

"It must be re-written," said Zul.

"Do we really need them all?" asked Erif. "This is just from Raef's youngling seasons. It does not even reveal anything of Black Rock."

"But it does reveal how Rail deceived the youngling into trusting it," said Zul, "It must be restored."

"You mean, re-written," said Erif, "and there are likely others that will need to be recreated as well."

Erif finished unrolling the three scrolls, laying stones out so they could dry. He returned to camp, retrieving scrolls and carrying them to higher ground to dry. He unrolled thirteen in all. The remnants of two scrolls remained in the crate, as they had been reduced to slush, floating at the bottom.

"Which two are we missing?" asked Zul, as Erif lay out the last scroll to dry.

"Let me see," said Erif, "I tried to lay them out in order."

He fingered the parchments, one nearly dissolving at his touch.

"I will need to re-write at least three of these," he said, "then somehow remember what the missing ones said and write them over from memory."

"Not from memory," said Zul, "we will watch the visions again, through the water. Have you found which are missing?"

"Yes," said Erif, "One was of Raef and Naan searching for the Soul Healer, I believe through their first season in Promise. The other was much older, from when Raef returned to Black Rock, after trying to escape."

Erif stood and gazed up at the clear sky.

"I do not want to see Black Rock again, Zul," said Erif.

"Nor do I," said the spirit, "but it must be done."

"All this to do," said Erif, his hands spreading wide, "and any sunrise the Neaverling will return to attack again."

"Think encouraging thoughts," said Zul, "when you return to the Great Province, perhaps you could acquire a position as a scribe."

"A Warrior-Scribe," said Erif, turning to Zul with a grin, "I am sure all the villages are looking for one of those."

—·◇·—

"Are you ready?" Raef asked Naan.

"I am," she replied, kissing him, "It will be a grand adventure."

Raef followed his wife and daughter from their little hut outside.

The sun had not been up long, but already it was warm. Most of the community was outside as well, preparing to leave or send off the caravan. Three older greenlings ran from the stable to meet them.

"The horses are all tied to the wagons," said one of the greenling, "just like Raef showed us."

"And all the provisions were packed sunset last," said Siro. "It appears you are ready to be on your way."

"As ready as we will be," said Raef.

Raef watched Ian push through the crowd toward him. "I may not have supported you much," said the elder, "but I do hope you meet success."

"Thank you," said Raef, "we will do our best."

There was an awkward silence.

"We should get started," said Naan.

The entire community left the huts, walking over the barren dust that had been the crop field, and out behind the stables where the carts were. Three newly built wagons stood full of pots, furniture and new clothing. Raef and Naan's smaller cart was in the lead carrying provisions.

Raef and Naan sat with Nine in the lead cart. Ura and Iris took the second wagon. Wynn, Bolin's wife, and Tren took the third and Jesson and Ramey took up the rear in the last wagon. The remainder stayed in Promise to hunt and take care of the young ones. Nine was the only youngling in the caravan.

Raef drove his cart past the field and huts to the faint trail that led back to the villages of the Great Province. They had not gone far down the path before the undergrowth blocked the way completely.

"Jesson!" called Raef, "Come help me clear a path. The trail has grown over!"

Raef and Jesson worked with swords to slice away the small branches and bushes. There was no need to get the axe out as no trees had fallen across the trail.

"This will be slow going," said Jesson, as he hacked away more limbs.

"I fear we will have to clear a path all the way to the main road," said Raef. "This will take an eternity."

Jesson laughed, "It is better than laying around back in Promise."

The band stopped at mid sun to eat. There was no place for to purge under the dense trees so they continued on. It was nearly sunset when they reached the end of the trail, where it met the fist intersection.

"I had forgotten there was more than one trail before the main road," said Raef.

"I think we go left from here," said Naan from behind.

"I believe you are correct," said Raef, "but we will need to camp here for now. The sun is too low to continue."

They men set up tents while the women cooked up a pottage for last meal. Nine ran in circles around the wagons, singing bright songs.

"If only we had such enthusiasm," said Ura, motioning to Nine.

They gathered to eat, sitting in a circle.

"I am disappointed we have traveled so little in a full sun's journey," said Jesson.

"We will go further next sun," said Raef, "This trail looks wide enough to travel without cutting a path for the wagons."

"I hope you are right," said Iris.

After last meal they retired early to their tents. Raef found it difficult to sleep. Nine woke often from the noises of the forest, waking him or Naan. Insects buzzed in his ear. The ground was hard and lumpy. When he did sleep, the sun returned too early.

"I will be glad when this is over," he said to Naan at sunrise, "so we can sleep on a straw mattress again."

"I concur," she said.

The caravan continued after first meal, turning left and heading northwest down the trail. By mid sun they reached the main road—Darkwood Trail. Raef turned his wagon due west.

"Will we reach the turnoff to Fir Hollow before sunset?" asked Naan.

"I cannot recall how far it is," said Raef, "Our first journey down this road was three seasons past."

"I hope we do not come across marauders as we did on our first journey," said Naan.

"We have four carts," said Raef, "and four men with swords. I think they would leave us be if they have any sense."

At three quarter sun they passed the trail that lead north to Fir Hollow.

"Perhaps we could stop here and sleep in Fir Hollow," said Naan. "We know enough people to find lodging for everyone."

"I am not ready to go back home quite yet," said Raef. "There are too many memories I do not wish to recall. We have tents. Besides, if we keep moving we can reach Midland sooner."

They stopped to camp where Darkwood Trail crossed Midland Road. They took the wagons well into the trees to get out of sight of the many travelers on the highway.

"Are we close?" asked Iris. "I have not been outside of Promise since I had only sixteen seasons, more than half a life past. I am eager to see a big city."

"From what I can remember," said Ura, "Midland is nothing more than a lot of noise."

"When were you in a Midland?" asked Raef.

"I was only a youngling," said Ura, "I do not recall why my family was there, I only remember the noise."

Raef found it more difficult to sleep than sunset past. The sharp click of hooves from the occasional traveler woke him several occasions. Nine and Naan, however, snored easily by his side.

The next sun was uneventful. They camped on Midland Road the following sunset and reached Midland City mid sun next. Raef found his backside quite sore from sitting on a bouncing wooden bench so long.

They found a spot at the end of one of a long row of merchant stalls to line their wagons up. They had no canvas to put up for shade, but the new wagons looked nice and attracted several shoppers right away.

Naan burst into the crowd, took the arm of a stylishly dressed woman, and pulled her to their wagons.

"Come, look at these dresses!" Naan said.

The woman's face grew tight, until Naan held up a blue and gray dress. The beadwork sparkled in the summer sun.

"My, where did you find this?" asked the woman,

her face softening.

"We make them in our village," said Naan, pointing to Wynn and Ura.

As the woman began to look through dresses a man with shoulder length hair walked up to a row of intricately carved bowls Tren had set up.

A Merchant, Raef thought, *and a wealthy one by the way he is dressed.*

"You will find nothing like these elsewhere in Midland," said Raef to the Merchant.

The man took a bowl with one hand, lifted it, and then nearly dropped it. He immediately brought his second hand to the bowl.

"These are heavy," said the Merchant. He held up the bowl, turning it in the sun. "Why, these are carved from solid rock!"

"Yes," said Tren, coming to the man's side, "Each bowl requires many suns to carve and polish."

"I thought these were glazed clay when I saw them," said the Merchant. "But this, this is quite extraordinary."

By sunset they had sold a third of all they had brought.

"I think our prices are too low," said Naan. "Otherwise we would not be selling so quickly."

"We cannot raise prices now," said Raef, "Everyone would be angry when they found out what we sold our wares for today."

"Sure we can," said Naan, "and if no one buys, we can move on to another city or village."

"Move on?" said Ura, "Again? I am not certain I want to keep travelling."

"Let us just see what happens next sun," said Jesson.

They camped in the wagons and were woken before sunrise by the noises of other Merchants preparing for market.

"I suppose you may raise the prices a bit," Raef announced at first meal.

"Stupendous!" said Naan, who put down her bowl and rushed to the street.

"She cannot possibly expect to sell anything so early," Raef mumbled.

"I think she already has," said Ura, looking over her shoulder.

Raef stood up and saw Naan taking money from a group of men as she handed over three rock bowls to them. He put his food down and rushed to Naan's side, just as the men were leaving.

"How much did you raise prices?" he whispered to her.

"I doubled them," she replied.

"You what!"

By mid sun they had sold half of all they had. Raef counted enough money to buy produce to last Promise until summer next.

"This is astonishing!" said Ramey, "I never imagined such fortune."

"Nor did I," said Raef.

They sold little the rest of the sun's journey, but continued to get high prices for what they did sell.

"We should pack up and continue south down the highway," said Naan, as they packed up what was left.

"Naan," said Raef, "Ura said she did not want to

travel farther. We should just return to Promise"

"Well," said Ura, standing up after eating, "I have changed my mind. I am an old woman and may not have many seasons left for travel. I am ready for adventure!"

The caravan packed up and returned to Midland Road the next sunrise. They headed south, travelling two full suns before coming to a vast grassy river delta and the village of Salt Marsh.

"What is that…that big blue in the distance?" asked Iris.

"I believe that is the ocean," said Naan. "I remember hearing that Salt Marsh is spread out between many rivers and lies near the sea."

"I have never seen the sea," said Ura. "Now I am very glad I came on this journey. I will see the ocean before my husband!"

Salt Marsh did not have plank built homes as would a true city, but it was vast for a village. It was mid sun before they found the village market. They set up their wagons and waited for customers. It did not take long for word to spread. Villagers came in flocks to see the wares of the mysterious village hidden between the mountains.

It was near sunset when a brightly dressed Noble, along with several Merchants, approached Jesson.

"Are you the Merchant representing the mountain village?" asked the Noble.

"No," said Jesson, pointing to Raef, "Raef speaks for us."

Raef approached the Noble and his band of Merchants, bowing slightly.

"An Intercessor Merchant?" asked the Noble.

"Intercessor?" said Raef, reaching back to feel his hair, "Well, not exactly. It is difficult to explain. I was once an Intercessor. I suppose I am acting as Merchant now."

The Nobles eyebrows lifted, "Peculiar culture, your mountain village has. It matters not to me," he said with a flick of his hand, "How much, for all that is left?"

Raef's eyebrows were next to rise. He felt himself quiver. He had some experience dealing with Nobles back in Fir Hollow, but Salt Marsh dwarfed his home village and this Noble was dressed in wealth he had not seen before. *How much are these men willing to pay?* He wondered. One of the Merchants spoke before Raef could.

"I see you fear we cannot afford such luxury," said the man, "I assure you that is not so."

"Let us spare you the task of seeking out buyers for your wares," said the Noble. He waved to one of the Merchants surrounding him.

The Merchant stepped forward and handed Raef a heavy cloth bag. Raef peered inside to find it full of gold coins. Raef stood speechless.

"Not enough?" asked the Noble. He waved to another Merchant, who handed another heavy bag to Raef.

"That…that is enough," stammered Raef.

Raef turned to the others by the wagons, "Stop selling! I have sold everything to these fine men."

Naan gave him a stern look. Raef motioned for her silence. She did not appear happy, but she stepped aside from the wagons. The Merchants hooked their horses to the last wagon full of goods and drove it away.

"Raef, what have you done?" asked Naan.

Jesson, Ramey, Ura, Iris and Tren gathered around. Raef opened the bags of gold for them.

"Raef!" said Naan, "how did you manage that?"

"I have no idea," said Raef.

Then Raef looked up to face Tren, smiling slowly.

"Did I not tell you your work would be prized?" asked Raef.

"I…I do not know what to say," said Tren.

"We will not starve!" said Ura, taking one of the bags of gold.

"No," said Raef, "we will indeed not starve."

28

They began purchasing food the next day. Less than half their money was spent before the remaining two wagons were full.

"We have more money," said Jesson, "and we need at least a little more produce."

"But we have no way to get it to Promise," said Iris.

Raef stood by the busy street, leaning against his small cart. A well-constructed wagon drove by, pulled by four sturdy horses.

"We shall simply purchase another wagon," said Raef.

"Buy a wagon?" asked Naan, "but, Raef, wagons are expensive."

Raef did not respond, but held up a bag of gold and shook it, his eyes smiling.

They bought three wagons and two more horses. The last wagon they loaded with smoked meats and wine.

"We might as well feast when we arrive in Promise," said Raef. "It would be a shame to let the money go unused."

Sunrise next they set off for the journey home.

The third sun of their journey, a band of horsemen rode slowly by the caravan. Raef pulled his sword slowly from its scabbard, rotating the silver blade in the sun. The lead man squinted at Raef, then snapped his reigns and rode quickly by. The other horsemen followed.

The fifth sun after leaving Salt Marsh, they reached Promise.

"Promise!" yelled Raef, as his small band emerged from the trail. He could see the back of Siro's hut first, just as he and Naan had when they first arrived.

"Siro, my old friend!" he yelled again, "Where are you? We have returned!"

Raef heard yelps from behind as his band of travelers celebrated. He laughed to hear Ura whooping the loudest. Iris came dashing past him, holding her dress up as she ran.

"What in all of the Province is going on?" came Ian's voice as he rounded Jesson's hut. Evot and a dozen younglings followed him.

"We have returned," said Raef, waving a hand toward the carts behind him.

Ian stopped in his tracks, his jaw dropping.

"What..." stammered Evot, "Where did you get all this?"

Jesson and Ramey's wives came round next, running to their husbands.

Ura got off her wagon and ran to hug Ian.

"You old goat," she said, "looks like you were wrong about Raef's plan."

"But, six wagons?" said Ian, "you left with four."

"Yes," said Ura, kissing him, "I am happy to see you remember how to count."

"Would anyone like a ham?" asked Jesson, holding up a smoked ham hock.

"What is a ham, Daddy?" asked a youngling, clinging to Jesson's leg.

Swarms of younglings and greenlings appeared, circling the carts and picking at the food. Garma finally dismounted her wagon, three bottles of wine tucked in her arm. Evot ran to kiss her.

They had a great feast at sunset by the fire pit.

"It will take all of harvest season to dry and store all this food," Ian said to Raef as they sat by the fire.

"It appears we have nothing else to do," said Raef, "since we have no harvest of our own."

"And no need to hunt," said Siro, "for at least a moon cycle or two. I was not expecting you to bring back meat."

Raef smiled, lifting his mug of ale.

"I must admit," said Ian, "I did not expect anything like this."

"And just imagine," said Raef, "we will have even more to sell next season. We can work all winter to till all six carts with goods to sell."

Ian's expression grew dark. He looked into the fire, sighed, and then looked back at Raef.

"Raef," said Ian, "I do not wish to repeat this again. We live a simple life here, and want to keep it that way. And, while all this may have been necessary this season, we do not want to become used to such extravagance."

"But, Ian," said Raef, "Think of what we could do. We could buy better tools to rebuild our huts. We could make roofs that withstand snow. We could buy livestock. We could buy plows to improve planting in the spring."

"Enough," said Ian, holding up his hand. "This is why we do not leave Promise. We do not want such outside influences. You did save us this season, I am forced to admit. But we do not want this to become a new way of life."

"We?" asked Raef, "Or do you really mean you? Everyone had a grand time in Midland and Salt Marsh. I am not sure all of Promise would agree with you."

"I am the elder here," said Ian, "and Promise follows my counsel."

Ian stood and walked to his hut. Raef felt his mouth fall open.

"What is it?" asked Naan, coming to his side.

She handed a sleeping Nine to him. He hugged his daughter to his chest.

"Ian does not want us to travel again," said Raef. "I do not understand him."

"Do not worry about it, husband. It has been a fine adventure, even if it was only once."

He leaned to her and she kissed him.

"And we have more adventures ahead," she continued.

"In what way?" he asked.

"I am pregnant again," said Naan. "We are going to have a second youngling."

"Another?" said Raef, sitting back so far he nearly

fell off the log he sat upon.

"Yes," said Naan. "I love you, Raef. I am happy I stayed here with you."

29

Erif carefully inked the last two lines of the re-written scroll, put the quill aside, and then stood up to stretch.

"Bending over so long is not kind to my back," he said.

"But you have completed one of the ruined scrolls," said Zul.

"I still have three more to do. And I have yet to construct a better chest to keep them in."

"And find a safer place to hide the chest," said Zul.

"This is not cheering me up," said Erif, grinning at the spirit.

"Come, let us walk a while," said Zul. "It will help your back."

Erif trailed Zul up a hill to an outcropping of boulders. The spirit walked a gap in the rocks and Erif followed to a hidden inner circle within. A small pool of water was at the center, shaded by the tall rocks surrounding it. Two smaller rocks were near the water's edge, each the perfect size for sitting upon.

"Why do I have the feeling you want to show me something?" said Erif.

"Raef's journey is not finished," said Zul, "and there is more to be recorded."

Erif sighed, sitting on one of the smaller rocks.

"Do I not need to continue training?" the Warrior asked. "The Neaverling will return. And I will face Rail in the future."

"I am minding those events," said the Great Spirit, "right now we need to check on our friend in Promise."

Zul stepped to the water's edge, waving a hand over it and causing the pool to ripple.

"We will move forward two seasons," said Zul, "Raef has reached twenty five seasons."

"Daddy!" said a small, male youngling, running from the hut toward Raef.

"Luffil!" said Raef, "Come, let us go see if the wagons are ready."

Luffil ran to Raef, who scooped him into his arms.

"We goin' on a trip?"

"A big trip," said Raef, "to the big cities up north."

Raef paused, looking at the community that had been his home the last five seasons. Tren's hut, at the far end, was many times its original size. Tren had married last season, a woman from Crest Ridge they had met while selling their wares. He had become quite wealthy, selling his stoneware throughout the villages and cities of the southern Province.

There were now eleven huts, two more than before. Evot's eldest son had married Bolin's eldest daughter and had a hut behind Evot's hut. Evot's second son had married Ian's second daughter, and they had built a hut behind Ian's. Ian's eldest daughter had married a man from Salt Marsh and had moved away. She had been the first to ever leave Promise and it had brought great sadness to the isolated community.

Raef heard a noise and turned to see Naan and Nine emerge from their hut. Raef had rebuilt his hut a season past and it was now quite large. Nine had grown tall for her nearly six seasons. She was graceful, even for a small youngling.

"Is everything ready?" asked Naan.

"Luffî and I were about to go see," said Raef.

"Shall we go with Daddy to see the wagons?" Naan asked Nine.

"Yes, yes!" Nine replied, jumping into the air.

Raef carried Luffîl as Naan and Nine walked by his side. They passed through the crop field, dark green leaves brushing their legs, some half as tall as Nine. Raef could hear commotion and talking from behind the barns as they approached.

Raef rounded the barn to see Ian leaning on a cane, pointing and giving orders as the others finished packing up the wagons. There were now nine large wagons, four horses pulling each.

"Good sunrise to you," said Ian, nodding to Raef.

"And to you," said Raef. "It appears everything is

ready."

"In spite the fact we asked you not to make another trip this season," said Siro, coming to Raef's side.

"I only said I was going again and others could come if they wanted," said Raef.

Ian looked down at the ground, his expression growing dark.

Raef put his son down and watched the youngling spring away, running to pet one of the horses on the nose. Nine followed.

"I do not mean disrespect," said Raef, quietly. "This is something I am good at. It has helped Naan and I survive here much easier. I am no good at hunting or gardening. I am good at selling."

"Selling what we make," said Siro.

"Excuse me," said Naan, "But I make much of what we sell."

"If you never sell," said Raef, "your artistry only piles up and is eventually thrown out. What does this hurt?"

"I lost my daughter to another village," said Ian. "She met her husband on one of your damned excursions."

"Ian, this happens in any village," said Raef, "our younglings grow up. Promise is too small for all of them to find a spouse here."

"Raef may be correct about this," said Siro, "eventually we will grow beyond what we are able to feed."

There was an uncomfortable silence. Naan left the men, walking to a group of woman.

"And we are getting old," said Siro. "You were unable to come on the last hunt, Ian. You will not be able to labor forever."

"My sons are strong greenlings," said Ian, "They can care for me."

Raef started to point out that his eldest son would likely marry soon and have younglings of his own to care for. He decided to remain silent.

"You had better be off," said Ian, "you have a long journey."

"Are you really planning on going all the way to Summit City?" asked Siro.

"It is no further than we have gone before," said Raef, "only in the opposite direction. To keep our prices high, we need to visit places that have not seen our craftsmanship. There are only so many people with enough wealth to pay what we ask. I imagine we have nearly used up those resources in the south."

Raef paused for Siro to respond, but the older man looked away. Raef gathered his family. They took the third cart, allowing Evot's eldest son to take the lead wagon. Raef had noticed the younger adults did not share their parent's pessimism toward the Merchant way of life.

The caravan was noisy with people singing loudly as they travelled. The path from Promise to Darkwood Trail had been cut wide and was no longer slow to travel. Seven couples and four older greenlings drove the wagons, with several younglings along for the ride. In total, nearly half the population of Promise had chosen to join the voyage.

On the second mid sun of the journey Raef

stopped the procession.

"Why are we stopping?" asked a greenling of fifteen seasons. He had been driving the front wagon.

"I see a clearing beyond the trees on both sides of the road," said Raef, "and the Dragon Children have not purged for nearly two suns. The men can use one side and the women the other. The rest of you can prepare mid sun meal."

The greenling's face reddened and he looked down, "Sorry, sir Raef. My father is a Dragon Child and I should have thought of that."

"No embarrassment is necessary," said Raef, "You were not a Dragon Child yourself. It is not yours to remember such things."

The greenling looked up at Raef, "It is necessary to...you know...purge, even when on a journey like this?"

"It is more necessary than at home," said Raef. "The excitement of a journey can cause us to be reckless. We are far from home and Rail roams freely here. We dare not take chances."

Raef gathered the men and began to walk through the trees.

"Where is Tren?" he asked Evot.

"Tren said he was not coming," said Evot, "he is helping his wife prepare food."

"Tren worries me," said Ramey, "every since he married he has been negligent with his purging."

"He says he does not feel the pull of Rail since he married," said Jesson.

"I am the newest among you," said Raef, "and even I know better than that."

After purging and mid sun meal they continued down Darkwood Trail.

"I think we are close to the road to Fir Hollow," said Naan, as she sat beside Raef.

"What is Fir Hollow?" asked Luffil.

"It is where Daddy and I were born," said Naan, tussling his wispy hair.

"And me too," said Nine.

"Yes," said Naan, "you were born in Fir Hollow, but we moved to Promise when you were still an infant."

"We will be traveling through Fir Hollow," said Raef, "to get to the northern cities."

"We are?" asked Naan, "I thought you would go around it. You had said you did not want to return there."

"To go around would require several suns journeys out of our way," said Raef. "Besides, I believe it is time we face our home village again."

"I must say," said Naan, "I am excited to hear that. I have not seen my mother for five seasons."

"That is why I plan for us to stay for a sun or two," said Raef, "the others can try to sell a bit in the market. We can visit our families. They have not even seen Luffi yet."

"Who did not see me?" asked the youngling.

"Your grandparents," said Naan.

"What is a gran-parents?" asked Luffil.

"We will explain it to you on the way," said Naan.

"I must admit I am anxious about seeing the Keepers," said Raef. "I was never clear if they knew I was a Dragon Child. I did many terrible things in Fir

Hollow. And what of my old friend, Chaz? He is a Warrior, likely a decorated one now. If he found out he would likely slay me on the spot."

Naan held his hand.

"Zul did not take us this far to have us slain," she said.

"I wish I had your faith," said Raef.

Raef saw the lead wagon reach the turnoff to Fir Hollow. He whistled and the lead driver looked back. Raef motioned for him to turn north. The caravan turned right and headed for Raef's home village.

Part Six

Home and Beyond

30

The tavern was shabbier than Raef remembered it.
The inn behind sagged a little. Raef entered the
tavern with Evot and scanned for the innkeeper. The
scent of sausage hung in the air as Raef gazed over
the rows of tables and benches where he had
celebrated Youngling's End and met the greenlings he
would come to live with in the Intercessor Dormery.
It seemed a lifetime past, another world he recalled
through foggy visions.

"Can I help you, fine sir?" asked a broad, squat
man behind the bar.

Raef recognized the innkeeper immediately,
though he could not recall his name.

"We need lodging, for a rather large party," said
Raef.

"We be almost empty," said the innkeeper, "so
you be in luck…why it be Keeper Raef!"

The man waddled up to Raef, reached up and
clapped his shoulders.

"Did not recognize you at first," the man said, "til
I saw your hair."

"I am not a Keeper any longer," said Raef. "I am, well, sort of a Merchant now."

"Merchant?" laughed the innkeeper, "A Intercessor who's a Merchant. What strange thing that be."

"We need beds for fourteen adults," said Raef, "the rest can sleep on the floor. Do you have room?"

"I thinks I can find room for you," said the innkeeper, "you got money for all that?"

"I am certain we can find an agreeable price," said Evot, "we have come prepared."

Raef left Evot with the innkeeper and returned to the others. He gathered the people of Promise and met the innkeeper in the inn. The round man showed them to their rooms. Raef stayed only long enough to see everyone would have room to sleep.

The wagons could be stored behind the inn but there were not enough stables for all the horses. Raef collected the men and greenlings and let the horses to the center of Fir Hollow.

Raef noticed the greenlings were wide eyed as they crossed the creek into the Labor sector. Filthy younglings ran unattended in the streets, some relieving themselves in the sewage ditches that lined the roads. A drunken man staggered down a narrow lane, only to fall face down in the mud. No one came to his aide.

"You have never seen where the Labor class live, have you?" Raef asked the greenlings of Promise.

"Why do they not clean this part of the village?" asked one of Bolin's sons.

"They are tired after hard labor each sun," Raef

replied, "they go home and rest rather than clean."

"It stinks here!" said another greenling.

"Yes, it does," said Raef. "And always has to my recollection."

"Did you live here?" asked Bolin's son.

"No," said Raef, "I lived in the Intercessor sector. It is clean, like Promise, on the other side of the village."

He chose not to mention that his wife, Naan, had lived in this sector before they were married. She could tell them if she chose.

They came to the Merchant stables, at the far southern edge of the Labor sector. The stable had room for all the horses and a fair price for the service was agreed upon. They all returned to the inn save for Raef, who took his wife and younglings, heading east into the Intercessor sector.

"This is so big!" shouted Luffi.

"Speak a bit softer, son," said Naan, "this part of the village is to be quiet."

"Why is that man in a robe?" asked Nine, pointing at an older greenling in a long, blue robe.

Naan cupped her hand over Nine's finger, pulling her hand down.

"Nine," said Naan, "we need to look down when a man passes by."

"But, why, Mommy?" said Nine, "I want to see his funny clothes."

"Remember last summer, when we went to Crest Ridge?" asked Naan. "And you and I had to look at the ground when men passed by?"

"Mommy, that is just silly," said Nine.

"It may be," said Raef, "but we must do as these villagers do when we are in their home."

Raef felt his heart speed up as he passed the Ceremonial Lodge. He could see the Dormery where he spent his thirteenth season. The memories of living away from his parents for the first time became fresh in his mind.

Young Intercessors in tan robes were gathering outside the Dormery, likely to be sent to late sun duties. A Keeper in a red robe approached the greenlings. Raef hurried his family past.

His parents' hut appeared much smaller than he recalled. It was in good order, however, with fresh white paint on the walls and a newly thatched roof.

"Father!" called Raef from the street, "Mother, it is your son, Raef!"

The door opened and Raef looked upon his mother. Her hair was graying and her face had become wrinkled. His heart skipped at the sight of her.

"Raef," said Malta, "Raef, you are home!"

"Yes, mother," said Raef, "as well as my family."

Malta ran to him, holding her hands up and cradling his face.

Raef hugged his mother and turned to his family behind him.

"You remember my daughter, Nine," said Raef.

Nine hid half behind Naan.

"Come, Nine," said Naan, "this is your grandmother, Daddy's mother."

Malta dropped to her knees, crying and holding out her arms. Naan coaxed Nine to Malta, who embraced the youngling.

"Why is my gramma crying?" asked Luffil.

"She is just happy to see Nine," said Raef, "it has been a very long time."

"Will she cry when she hugs me?" asked Luffil. "She never sees me before at all."

"This is your son?" asked Malta, still on her knees.

Raef led Luffil to his mother. Luffil smiled and held his arms up to Malta.

"I am the grana-son," Luffil announced.

Malta lifted Luffil and hugged him.

"That is kinna hurting me," said Luffil, "but I knows you not be trying to hurt me."

Malta stood, still holding Luffil, tears in her eyes.

"Come, come in," Malta said. "Folor will be home in a bit."

They sat on benches around the cooking fire. Malta kept Luffil on her lap and the youngling seemed pleased to remain there. Nine sat between Raef and Naan, still looking quite sheepish.

"I want to know everything that has happened," said Raef.

"Yes," said Naan, "how is everyone?"

"Your sister, Mira, has two more younglings," said Raef's mother, "her husband, Wren, has become the Master of the Masons Guild. They are doing very well."

"It will be good to see her again," said Raef.

His mother looked aside, her smile fading.

"I do not know if she will see you," said Malta. "She knows about…you know."

"The dragon," said Raef, "she knew about that before I left Fir Hollow."

Malta looked at Nine and her face grew red.

"Mother," said Raef, "we do not hide such things from our younglings. To do so makes them vulnerable, not safe."

Malta took a deep breath.

"I suppose you may be right," she said, "I wish we had talked to you more about…that. Perhaps you would not have become prey to…it."

"That is in the past," said Raef, "you were not alone in keeping silent about such things. All of Fir Hollow refused to speak of Rail."

His mother's face grew brighter red at the word.

"I am sorry for being so blunt," said Raef, "but the way to safety from the dragon is not through secrecy."

"I know you are right," said Malta.

"Why will my sister not see me?" asked Raef, "She knew about me seeing the dragon before. It was she who suggested I go in search of a Soul Healer."

"And we found him," said Naan, "it has been wonderful what he has done for us."

"Your sister," said Malta, sighing deeply, "she revealed something to us a season after you and Naan left. When she was a greenlia, a greenling that fancied her took her to see…the dragon."

"What?" said Raef, standing up. "Mira went to see the dragon? I can scarcely believe it."

"It was against her will," said Malta, "and she suffered greatly from the secret she kept from us."

"I can only imagine," said Raef, "but this gives me

more reason to want to see her. We have much to discuss."

"Raef, you took others to see the dragon," said Malta, "You remind Mira of the one who betrayed her by taking her to the dragon."

Raef sat, stunned at his mothers words.

"She is angry," said Malta. "I will speak to her, but I fear she will not see you."

"Who is Mira, Mommy?" asked Nine.

Malta began to cry. Luffil looked up at his grandmother, then turned to face her and hugged her. Malta hugged the small youngling close.

"There is more, Raef," said his mother, "More that I need to tell you. You see I know the dragon as well. My father took me to see it when I was just a youngling."

Raef felt his blood run cold.

"Raef," said his mother, "I have been to Black Rock."

31

Raef walked through the streets of the Intercessor sector in a daze.

My own mother has been to Black Rock, he thought. *I cannot even imagine it. How did I not know?*

He recalled the time she found a dragon hair on his clothing. All the times he came home late.

She had to have known, he realized, *perhaps living at Black Rock explains why she reacted so little to my obvious involvement with Rail.*

He knew it was wise to learn more of his family's history with dark spirits, but it was too much to hear so soon.

I told Mother I would fetch Father, he thought, *but I am not eager to return home.* He took the long way to The Keep, looping around the Ceremonial lodge on the way.

Raef passed the Intercessor stables and noticed a young man leaning against the wall. Raef looked again. There was something oddly familiar about his face. Then Raef recognized him; he had the face of the youngling who grew up in the hut next to his.

"Nilo, is that you?" Raef asked.

The young man snapped his head around to look at Raef. His mouth drooped, then melted into a grin.

"My old friend, Raef," said Nilo, "so, you have finally returned to us."

Raef ducked into the shadow of the stable, next to the young man. Nilo was quite thin and still had the face of a greenling, though he must have twenty seasons by now. His straw hair went past his shoulders, as any Intercessor's would. His tan tunic was tattered and unkempt, which struck Raef as strange on this side of the village. It was hard to imagine that this young man was once the annoying youngling who pestered Raef as a greenling, begging for attention. The youngling who Raef finally took to see Rail, once Raef's own friends refused to go any longer.

"It is good to see you," said Raef.

"You are not wearing a Keeper's robe," said Nilo, looking skyward.

"I am not a Keeper," said Raef, "not even an Intercessor any longer. I am not qualified to be so."

"After you brought half the Intercessor sector to be seduced by Rail," said Nilo, "it is well that you can admit that."

"Half?" said Raef. He repressed the desire to defend himself. "I suppose you, in particular, have reason to loathe me."

"I do not hate you," said Nilo, looking down at his worn shoes. "But I have never escaped what you did to me."

"I do not know how to undo my past," said Raef.

"I only did what was taught to me. If you remember DeAlsím, who was a greenling when we were younglings—it was he who first took me to Rail."

"That is no excuse!" spat Nilo, "I had far fewer seasons than you. I had no way to know what you were bringing me to."

Raef looked away. *I would give anything to go back, to make right what I did wrong.*

Nilo shifted his weight, still leaning against the stable, and looked blankly forward.

"I still go, now and then," said Nilo. "I tell myself I will not but a sun always comes when I do. That damned dragon pulls you in like a fish in a net."

"I know that feeling," said Raef.

"I left the Intercessor class," said Nilo, "just like you. I joined an acting troupe two seasons past. I am only here because we have a show in Fir Hollow."

"You joined a troupe?" asked Raef, "What in all the Province for? You were born an Intercessor. Even the lowest Intercessor is above most of the village in status. A roving player is below even the Labor class."

"What is that to you?"

Raef felt his face redden. *I am just making it worse*, he thought.

"I see you still wear your hair long," said Raef, trying to lighten the mood.

Nilo reached behind his back and fingered his locks.

"I will cut it," said the young man, "soon."

"Nilo," said Raef, "I have met someone who can help you. Naan and I found a Soul Healer. A Soul Healer can free one from the dragon's spell."

"I have had quite enough help escaping the dragon," said Nilo. "I went to the Keepers to help. I cannot believe I had the courage to tell them what I had done. They nearly evicted me from the village. Then Keeper Chaumer said he could help. He had me meditating every sun for a moon cycle."

Nilo spit on the ground, "The Keepers did nothing but shame me. They are of no use whatsoever."

"Nilo, this is not a Keeper at all. The Soul Healer is a Wizard."

"You went to see a Wizard?" asked Nilo. "You have less sense than I. No, I will have nothing to do with your Soul Healer. The magic of the Keepers is a hoax as would be any Wizard's magic. I am done with such nonsense."

"But, Nilo, I really am free from Rail's pull," Raef.

Nilo stood to face Raef, "Perhaps you are better than I. You always thought you were. Well, I am a simple player now. No one expects a member of an acting troupe to stay away from sordid spirits. I can do as I wish with no further shame."

"There is always shame," said Raef, "that comes from within."

"Be silent!" shouted Nilo, "This entire village is a fraud, Raef, and you know it. Do you have any idea how many consort with Rail?"

Raef stood, stunned at Nilo's rant.

"This whole village stinks of dragon," Nilo continued, "yet they all pretend disdain of it."

"I did not know Fir Hollow had sunk into depravity," said Raef. "But even so, there is a place where pretense truly has been done away with. I will take you if you like."

"Leave me be," said Nilo, waving Raef away, "go pretend with the others. I live with a band of people who do not pretend."

Raef stepped closer to Nilo, studying his face. Raef saw anguish and pain.

"Actors may be below even the Labor class in society," said Nilo, "but we know we are really no worse than any of you."

Raef watched the young man walk away.

"I am sorry," said Raef, "I am sorry for what I did to you."

Raef stumbled to the Keep, hoping to find his father there. He entered the door, and then remembered that it was forbidden to enter the Keep uninvited, lest one was a Keeper or Keeper's Apprentice.

A greenling in a blue robe was in the waiting room of the Keep. He looked up at Raef wide eyed, his mouth hanging open.

"My apologies," Raef stammered, "I forgot my place."

A man stepped through the curtain separating the waiting room from the Keepers hall. He wore the red robe of a Keeper. Raef recognized him.

"Who dares bust in…?" asked the man. The man's face softened as his eyes met Raef.

"Raef?" said the Keeper, "you have returned."

"Yes, Prime Keeper Bremmen," said Raef, "I am sorry for bursting in. I forgot that I am no longer…"

"Come, come," said Bremmen, "come sit with

me."

Raef sat on a bench with Keeper Bremmen. The greenling's eyebrows rose, but he remained silent.

"It has been many seasons," said Bremmen.

"I am only passing through," said Raef, "on my way north. I was looking for my father. I want him to meet my family."

"Apprentice," said Bremmen, "go fetch Keeper Folor."

The greenling skittered away.

"Where have you been?" asked the Keeper.

"Naan and I went in search of a Soul Healer," said Raef.

"I recall you rescinding your role as Keeper," said Bremmen, "and leaving us five seasons past."

"Keeper Bremmen, I must ask you a delicate question. You see, I went to seek a Soul Healer because I had become enslaved by…well…by a dragon."

"I suspected as much," said Bremmen, "you were very distant, even as a youngling. I had hoped becoming a Keeper would free you, but you only became more distant and isolated."

"You…you suspected?" asked Raef. "Why in all the Province did you not try to help me?"

Prime Keeper Bremmen looked at his feet.

"We do not speak of the dragon," said the elder Keeper, "it is strongly discouraged."

"That is just tradition," said Raef. "What good is tradition if it puts the village in danger? Do you even know what Rail truly does?"

Bremmen's face reddened at the dragon's name,

but he did not reprimand Raef for speaking it.

"You tell us that it kills and eats anyone who it finds," said Raef. "That is a lie! It only eats the dead."

"We know," said Bremmen.

"You know?" Raef stood up and began to pace in front of Bremmen. The Prime Keeper looked oddly meek.

"Do you also know it puts its prey into a trance?" said Raef. "Did you know it kidnaps its victims and takes them to Black Rock? Did you know there are hundreds of people living, right now, with the dragon, beyond the mountain's rim?"

"Raef," said Bremmen quietly, "we know. We know about Black Rock and the Great Basin within."

"Keeper Bremmen!" said Raef, "Those people are enslaved! There are hundreds, maybe thousands of them. Yet you pretend they do not even exist!"

Bremmen slowly stood, facing Raef. The older man's face looked weary.

"We do not speak of such things," said Keeper Bremmen, "it is forbidden to be recorded in our sacred scrolls. When one is lost to…the dragon, he or she never returns. It is useless to attempt to save them lest we be seduced ourselves. It is not so much a lie to say they have been killed."

"Do I look dead!" shouted Raef, "Was I lost forever to the beast? I have been to Black Rock, Prime Keeper, and I returned."

"We do not understand how that is possible," said Bremmen, "we thought you overcame it. That is why we made you a Keeper."

"But I was still under its spell," said Raef, "I did

more harm as Keeper than if you would have demoted me as you should have. It is not returning from Black Rock that made me free, it was the Soul Healer who did that."

Raef stilled himself, containing his rage. Prime Keeper Bremmen returned his gaze.

The door to the Keep opened and Folor entered with the apprentice.

"Keeper Folor," announced the greenling.

"Raef!" said Folor. "My son has returned!"

"We should go see mother," said Raef, "she is waiting with my family."

Folor stood before Raef, smiling. Raef thought his father was going to hug him, but instead Folor turned and walked out the door. Raef caught the door with his hand and turned to Bremmen.

"The Soul Healer, the one who freed me, is a Wizard," said Raef, "Perhaps the villages have been following the wrong guides all these generations."

32

Folor held Luffil on his knee, holding the youngling's shoulder at arms length. Malta was weeping softly, her tears glistening in the firelight. Nine play quietly in a corner, glancing now and then at the adults. Naan held Raef's hand.

"My father did not exactly take me to Rail," said Malta. "I was born at Black Rock. My parents had been taken when my mother was pregnant."

"I cannot even imagine such a thing," said Raef. "To know of nothing but Black Rock from birth. But, how did you get out?"

"It was not on purpose," said Malta, "when I was a greenlia I went exploring and followed a trail that lead out of the basin. I became lost and wandered many suns. I ran into your father in the forest, when he was out hunting. He took me home and we were married the following season."

Raef leaned back, trying to imagine what his mother had described.

"Did you know where Mother had been?" Raef asked his father.

"She told me," said Folor. "It was hard to believe, after what I had been taught about the dragon, but I came to believe her."

"You told me your parents were dead," Raef said to his mother. "Did they die before you left Black Rock?"

"As you likely know," said Malta, "families do not stay together in the Great Basin. I saw my parents occasionally, but they acted as if I were just another youngling. We were not a family."

"There are no families in Black Rock," agreed Raef.

"My parents were alive when I left them," Malta continued. "It was easier to tell you and your sister they were dead than explain about Black Rock. I have no idea if they still live."

Raef tried to recall the elders he met in Black Rock, wondering if any had been his grandparents.

"And you did not want to return to Black Rock?" Raef asked. "Most Dragon Children cannot be away from Rail long."

"Dragon Children?" asked Folor.

"What Rail's slaves are called," said Raef.

"I do not know that I was what you call a Dragon Child," said Raef's mother. "I did not choose to be with the dragon. The things of Black Rock were normal to me as a youngling, but I was not particularly drawn to Rail as I saw that others were."

"Did it lick you?" asked Raef.

"Did it what?"

"Lick you," repeated Raef, "with its long tongue. That is how it sedates its victims. It's saliva affects humans."

Malta shivered, "I never liked seeing that. It did it to all those in the Basin. I avoided it."

Raef turned to his father, "Why did you not tell anyone?"

"No one wanted to believe," said Folor.

"The Keepers appear to know," said Raef, "at least Prime Bremmen does."

"Yes," said Folor, "some do, but very few will admit this knowledge, even in secret."

"I tried to tell," said Raef's mother. "I told the Keeper of Crest Ridge before your father and I married. The Keeper became angry with me and said not to lie about such things. He nearly threw me out of the village. I did not dare speak of it again."

"So many secrets," said Raef.

"We should eat," said Folor, standing and placing Luffil on the ground. "It is not good to speak of evil for so long."

Raef helped pull the table into place. He had more questions for his parents but could see they were done speaking about the past.

Raef took his family back to the inn to sleep after last meal. He dreamed of Black Rock. In his dream he was trying to convince the Dragon Children to leave with him. Some said they did not believe he knew the way out. Others said they did not want to leave. Then Rail appeared in his dream and attacked him. Unarmed, Raef could only run and hide.

33

The image of Raef sleeping faded with the rippling water. Erif stood and walked back to camp. He unrolled a new parchment and retrieved his quill and ink, ready to record what he had seen. Then Erif stopped and glanced at his long sword.

"Are you not going to record the vision?" asked Zul, appearing next to Erif.

"Not now," said Erif, putting down his quill.

Erif unsheathed the sword and carried it up to a flat topped, rocky hill. The Great Spirit followed silently. Erif lifted the sword and swung it twice. His arms protested at the weight of the weapon.

"It has been too long since I have trained with my long sword," said Erif.

"The vision must be recorded," said Zul.

"Later," said Erif, swinging again.

"As you wish," said the spirit, "I will return in two suns."

The spirit vanished and Erif sliced the air,

trusting forward and upward.

"When I face you, Rail," Erif said, "I will not be unarmed."

"That is a steep road," said Evot.

Raef looked up the zigzag path leading up the rock face to Summit City above.

"The Overseers would not allow their city to be easily approached," said Raef.

"Well," said Evot, shifting in his seat, "it would certainly not be easy to attack from down here."

"I think we can make it before sunset if we begin now," said Raef.

"We had better," said Evot, "I do not see any place to stop and camp. The entire road appears to have a rock wall on one side and a cliff on the other."

Raef snapped the reigns and drove his wagon forward. He had taken the lead for the last leg of the journey, with Evot at his side.

It was the third sunrise after they had departed Fir Hollow. They had passed through Pine Creek and White Rock but stopped in neither village. Raef wanted to test their wares in Summit City. He imagined that the Overseers would be willing to pay higher prices than anyone else in all the Great Province.

The road was steep and taxed the horses, but it was smooth and well travelled. It was also surprisingly wide, allowing wagons to pass each other, which was fortunate as it was heavily travelled.

When they reached the plateau Raef paused the

horses. A stone wall rising higher than the trees rose abruptly before them. It was too wide to see around properly. A single arch was the only way in or out, at least on this side of the city. When they passed under the arch the road changed from dirt to flat, square-cut stone.

"Streets of cut stone!" said Evot, "who could afford such lavishness?"

"The Overseers, apparently," said Raef, trying to hide his own amazement.

Raef felt his jaw drop as they passed under the arch and entered the city itself. It looked as if everything was made of cut stone. The structures, every one of them, were constructed of a reddish stone and the streets of a nearly white rock. Streets wound off in all directions, not in straight lines as in the other villages. Many structures had two or three stories, with window openings all the way up. Along the streets there were canals of water, here and there terminting in pools of water contained by carved circles of stone. The plants that did grow sprouted from ceramic pots.

"What is this place?" Raef stammered.

"It feels to be the home of the Great Spirit himself," said Evot.

"The sun is setting," said Raef, "We must find lodging quickly. I do not see any place to camp. We will need to find an inn."

The wagons were lined up down one of the lesser-used alleys while Evot and his sons went in search of lodging. Raef found a stable for the horses, though it cost far more than he had expected. Evot returned soon to show the way to the inn.

"You will not fathom what it costs to sleep here," said Evot to Raef.

"I just paid the stable hand," said Raef, "I fear I will not be surprised."

Raef and his family got their own room on the second floor of the in. The polished wood floor was cold to Raef's feet.

"Come to bed, husband," said Naan, after bedding the youngling.

Raef lay on his back on the bed, which was a down-filled mattress on a raised wooden box. He studied the beams and planks above his head.

"I hope that is strong enough to keep whoever is sleeping above us from falling through," he said. "I do not entirely trust these buildings that stack people over each other."

"Hush, husband," said Naan, "they have lived like this for generations."

"And how many have died from collapsed inns in all those generations?" asked Raef.

He felt a slap on his arm.

"Ouch!" he said, "I was only joking. Mostly joking."

They woke before the sun and made first meal from their own provisions. Raef took Evot, Jesson, Ramey and Tren, along with samples of their work, to look for a spot to set up the wagons to sell.

"I do not see any markets," said Tren.

"I cannot see much at all," said Jesson. "These tall buildings and narrow streets make me feel like I am down some hole."

"Perhaps we should split up," said Raef, "we could find a market sooner. Jesson and Tren with me, Ramey with Evot."

Raef, Jesson and Tren came upon a market, but it was like none Raef had ever seen.

"It is inside!" said Tren. "Who puts a market inside?"

Raef looked at the structure, a series of stone arches supporting a large, flat roof. It was packed with vendors and buyers.

"Come," said Raef, "let us find a spot inside for our wagons."

But there was no spot. Well-constructed and rather permanent looking booths occupied every space.

"Where can we set up a booth?" Raef asked a well-dressed Merchant.

The Merchant gave Raef a sour look, "Unless you are a member of a Merchant Guild, you may not have a booth. Besides, all the booths have been leased for the next season."

"Sorry," said Raef, "we will look elsewhere."

"There is no elsewhere!" called the Merchant as they left. "Common villagers!"

Raef hurried out of the market, surrounded by laughter.

"Go find Evot and Ramey," Raef told Jesson and Tren, "tell them about this. I will look for the Council Hall. Perhaps it will be faster starting at the top."

"What do you know of the workings in a Council Hall?" asked Ramey.

"When I was a Keeper I had dealings with the

Nobles in the Council Hall in Fir Hollow," said Raef.
"How different could it be here?"

Raef watched his friends find their way down the
street. Then he turned the other way and walked to
what he hoped would be the center of the city.

He came across a towering structure, five stories
tall, with an elegant stone stairway leading to the
entrance.

This must be it, he thought.

He walked up the stone steps and entered
through two thick, oak doors, nearly twice his height.
The entry room was tall, the ceiling rising up two full
stories. Flowery dressed men walked here and there,
not even glancing at Raef.

He spotted a man in a dark robe, standing on a
stool and painting words on a large parchment pinned
to the wall. Raef tried to read it, though the dialect
seemed strange. It appeared to be a schedule or list of
events. He walked to the man, standing under him as
he inked out more words.

"Excuse me, scribe," said Raef, "I was wondering
if you could assist me."

The man paused, then looked down, his face
turning sour. He did not speak.

"Yes," said Raef, "I was speaking to you. I am
wondering, fine sir, if you could help me find a place
in this great city where we can sell our wares."

The man's eyebrows lifted.

"Sell…you wares?" the man said slowly. "Sir, I am
the chief scribe to the Overseers. I, nor anyone else in
the Great Hall, deal with such minutia."

"I apologize, sir," said Raef with a bow, "perhaps

you could direct me to someone who…"

"Who let you in?" said the scribe, coming down off his stool. His eyes widened once he was on the floor, looking up at Raef who was taller by a head than he.

"This is a hall of Nobles," said the scribe, "remove yourself at once."

"But, about the markets," said Raef.

"Are you a simpleton?" asked the scribe, "go find the Merchants Guild. Where else would you find permission to sell?"

Raef bowed and walked quickly for the door.

"Peasant," came the scribe's voice from behind.

Raef had to ask several people on the street before he found the Merchants Guild. From the way the scribe had spoken, Raef expected it to be a small building. The Merchant Guild Hall was shorter, but no less ornate or impressive than the Great Hall had been.

Raef pulled in a deep breath and walked inside. At once, every head in the entry room lifted to gaze at Raef.

"I was wondering…" Raef began.

Before he could speak further a well-dressed greenling approached him and pointed him down a hall. Raef followed the greenling to a room where two men sat at wooden desks. Parchments littered the finely oiled desktops.

"May I be of service?" asked one of the men.

"I am Raef, from the southern Province. I am here with a caravan of Merchants, looking to sell our wares here in Summit City. I was wondering…"

"Outsiders are not permitted to sell in our markets," said the second man.

"Not at all?" asked Raef.

"No," said the first, "especially village Merchants."

Raef sighed and turned to leave.

"You could try one of the shops," said one of the men. "They are more exclusive, but they purchase their goods from the cities below. Perhaps they would consider you."

The sun was mid sky when Raef left he Guild. He took two deep breaths, trying to fight off the gloom that was overtaking him.

He found a shop several streets away. He walked into the single story structure to find rows of tables covered in ornate ceramics and clothing. Some wooden furniture stood in a far corner. The shop owner approached Raef.

Raef held up one of Tren's rock bowls he had brought with him.

"You wish to sell me something, I take it," said the man. "I generally prefer it the other way around."

Raef grinned meekly and held out the gleaming bowl.

"The design is a bit unique," said the man, "but we have many that are similar."

The shop owner took the bowl. His hand immediately fell and he nearly dropped the bowl.

"Did you fill it with lead?" asked the shop owner, laughing.

"It is carved from rock," said Raef.

"Rock? Now, that is different. Ceramic and

precious metals I have seen, but not this."

The man turned the bowl over in his hands.

"We have beaded dresses and tunics," said Raef, "and carved furniture."

"Go see our furniture," said the man, "is yours any different?"

Raef walked to the benches and tables in the corner. He had to admit; the woodwork they had brought was no better.

"I have never seen this quality outside of Promise," said Raef. "In the southern Province, our wares are unique."

"They would likely be in the rest of the northern Province as well," said the shop owner, "but up here on the summit, we have the best craftsmen in all the Great Province."

"You do not try to sell elsewhere?" asked Raef.

"Some consider it sacrilege to sell our wares off the summit," said the shop owner with a laugh. "Not me, mind you, but some of the Guild Masters. They control all commercial activity on the summit."

"On the summit?" asked Raef. "Do you not mean Summit City?"

"Summit City and Krellit beyond."

"Krellit?" said Raef, "you mean, the city of learning?"

"Yes, where the philosophers and learned men study."

"My father studied in Krellit," said Raef, "with the cloudsmen. I never knew where the city was."

"Yes, that is very nice, I am sure," said the shop owner, "I will tell you what, young Merchant. I will purchase some of these rock carvings. Bring me what you have, but only if you give your word not to sell to any other shop in Summit City."

"And the garments and furniture?" asked Raef.

"Sorry," said the man, "we have no need for those."

Raef and the caravan departed Summit City two suns later, much lighter from selling all of Tren's goods, but disappointed to sell nothing else.

Raef rode with Naan and his younglings on the way down the summit.

"If we come back after only selling this," said Raef, "Ian will throw me out of Promise."

"We still have the northern villages to try," said Naan. "Besides, we cannot expect to sell out every summer."

"I hope you are right," said Raef, "but only about the villages. We cannot return selling so little. Ian will be furious."

34

Erif watched the water ripple, and then become calm. The image of Raef and Naan was gone.

"I must return to the Great Province," said Zul. "There is unrest I must tend to. I will not return again for over a moon cycle."

"I shall await your return," said Erif.

"You must continue your work," said Zul, "you cannot wait for my return."

"I have no ability to conjure visions," said Erif.

Zul bent over and picked up a piece of slender driftwood the length of Erif's forearm.

"Use this," said Zul.

As Zul held the stick, it began to glow blue.

Erif backed away, "I am no Wizard."

Zul smiled at him, extending the wand to Erif.

"No," said the spirit, "not a Wizard. You are a Warrior who carries my power."

Erif cautiously took the stick, turning it in his hand.

"I…I am afraid, Zul. I do not know how to use your power."

"You are ready," said the ancient spirit, "I trust you, you can trust yourself as well."

Erif held the wand out and it glowed brighter. He smiled and looked to Zul. The spirit smiled back, fading from sight.

————·◇·————

Raef, Naan and their younglings rode in the last wagon of the caravan. Raef could hear the yelling and celebrating ahead, where the front wagons had reached Promise.

"Are we home, Daddy?" asked Nine.

"Yes, daughter, we are home again."

Luffíl crawled from the back of the wagon, squeezing between Raef and nine on the driver's bench. Their wagon broke out of the trees and was instantly surrounded by younglings.

"Welcome home," said Siro, who walked to their wagon.

"It is good to be home at last," said Raef.

"At last is right," said Siro, "We expected your return a moon cycle past."

"It took longer this season," said Raef, "we were in unknown territory. But we did finally sell everything."

"The harvest suffered from lack of workers," said Siro. "The growing season has past and you were not here to help."

Raef studied Siro's face.

"Siro," said Raef, "we brought back more

vegetables than our little field ever produces."

"Never mind that now," said Siro, "it is nearing sunset. We will need to prepare food for everyone."

The sun was too low to prepare much of a feast, but everyone ate our around the fire pit. Raef noticed that Ian stayed on the other side of the fire and did not attempt to speak to him.

"I am concerned about Ian," said Raef to Naan.

"What is there to be concerned about?" she replied. "We did sell everything and brought back more food than ever, as well as a large profit."

"I do not think Ian cares about such things," said Raef.

"Daddy, my friends are all here!" announced Nine.

"Yes, they are. You should go play with them."

Raef watched his daughter skip away, followed by his son, still gnawing on a quail drumstick.

"It is good to be back," he said to Naan. "It was not good for Nine and Luffil to be stuck in a wagon for so many suns."

Naan leaned on his shoulder, "It is good to be back. It is so quiet here."

It took three suns to hang the vegetables they had purchased to dry and store the salted meats. Contrary to what Siro had said, there were still salvageable crops in the fields and Raef saw to it they were harvested. On the forth sun, Raef left Promise to hike up to the Wizard's hut. He arrived by three quarter sun.

"It is a surprise to see you," said Tup, upon Raef's arrival.

"We were away on our seasonal trading excursion," said Raef, "it took much longer than I anticipated."

"I was not remarking about that," said the wizard, "I knew you were away. I meant that you arrived so early in the sun's journey."

Raef smiled, "I suppose my legs have grown stronger over the seasons."

"Come," said Tup, "let us go to the summit."

"We usually wait until sunrise," said Raef.

"We usually do not have time before dark," Tup retorted.

Raef paced around the perimeter of the summit with Tup. It was completely silent, save for the sound of their feet upon the rock.

"It feels smaller," said Raef.

"Smaller?" asked Tup.

"This summit. It seems smaller than I remembered it."

Tup grinned, "A lot has changed for you. Do you still carry the stone I gave you?"

Raef pulled the leather pouch he always carried from his waist tie and held it upside down, dropping the stone into the Wizard's outstreached hand. The old man rolled it in his palm. Sunlight played off the blue surface. Raef noticed that one side was still slightly smudged with dirt.

"There is still a bit of dirt on it," said Tup, "but we all still have some cleaning to do. Yet, like this stone, real man inside is now visible. Most of what Rail did to you is gone."

Tup handed the stone to Raef and he held it up

to the sun. Light shone through it.

"I cannot thank you enough for what you have done for me," said Raef, "you and all those in Promise."

"You do not need me any longer," said Tup. "You still must continue purging, though little essence remains in you, and you must keep no secrets. But you no longer need a Wizard's assistance."

Raef walked to the eastern ledge, his boots at the edge, and looked down. The treetops were no more than a smear of green from so high.

"How is it going for you?" asked Tup

"It is odd," said Raef, "My wife loves me more than before she knew about my time with the dragon. The first two seasons here were hard for us, but now we are stronger than I could have hoped for."

"And your younglings?"

"They are amazing. So happy," said Raef. "And my work, who would have thought I would become a Merchant? And with such success. I have brought wealth to Promise it never knew before."

"Raef," said Tup, "I am pleased that you have seen success, but I think you are called to be something greater than a Merchant."

"My life is very good now," said Raef. "I would change nothing. But for a Keeper who betrayed his own village to be restored with such prominence, it is beyond anything I deserve."

Raef stepped back from the ledge, looking off to the east at the shadow that was Black Rock.

"I wish there was some means to repay what has been done for me," said Raef, "some way to help others, as I have been helped."

"Do you mean that?"

Raef spun around to see who had spoken, for it was not the voice of Tup.

"Zul!" said Raef, "I did not know you were here."

"Did you mean what you said?" asked the Great Spirit.

"Yes," said Raef, "yes I do. Yet I cannot think how I could help those enslaved by Rail. Even if I could, who would want help from someone who betrayed his own village?"

The Spirit smiled but said nothing in reply.

Raef returned to Promise two suns later, not long after mid sun. Naan, Nine and Luffil ran to meet him as he entered the circle of huts. He kissed each of them.

"Raef!" said Ian, walking to meet him. "We have not yet gone to purging. Will you join us?"

"Of course, old friend."

Raef walked with the men who had been Dragon Children, through the field and beyond the barns to the mound in the meadow where purging was done. He removed his tunic and undergarment to reveal a back covered in scars. The fall sun was warm, but not hot. A bit of essence glistened on his skin, but very little.

"Your merchant journeys have done well," said Ian, "far better than any of us imagined."

"Thank you," said Raef. "I only wanted to help the people who helped me for so many seasons."

"And we are grateful," said Siro.

"We see you have great talents," said Ian, "and I

am certain they would be highly valued in any village. But, you see, my friend, Promise needs to get back to what we were."

"What do you mean?" asked Raef.

"We are not a village of Merchants," said Siro.

"We are hunters and farmers," said Evot. "Some of us enjoyed these last three seasons selling our wares across the Great Province, but we are tired."

"We do not need wealth," said Ian. "If we have another drought, you have taught us a way to purchase food. We can always do that again. But until then, it is time for Promise to return to a slower pace of life."

"I hear your words, Ian," said Raef. "I do not entirely understand, but I accept them."

"There is more," said Siro.

"Raef," said Ian, "you no longer need to live in Promise. Your healing is sufficient for you to move elsewhere."

"And you are not meant for our pace of living," said Evot. "Many of us have lived here in Promise since our greenling seasons. This is all we know. All we want."

"We believe it is time for you and Naan to return to the villages," said Ian. "You are not meant to stay with us."

"You want me to leave?"

"Not want," said Siro. "It is what is best for you."

"Besides," said Evot, "while you can hunt now, it is not your passion. You are not a craftsman. With nothing to sell, what would you do here?"

Raef felt a tear on his cheek.

"I…I do not wish to leave," said Raef. "But as you say, I do not know what I would do if I stayed. Once the summer caravans have stopped, I do not know what I would do."

"Certainly not work in the fields!" laughed Siro. "We saw how that worked out."

"No," said Raef. "No, that would not be good."

"We know you will need money to start over," said Ian, "so we are giving you all the profit from your last excursion."

"All?" said Raef, "but, Ian, that is two season's wages!"

"We need no money here," said Siro. "It is expensive to live in a proper village. Especially outside of the Labor sector."

"And we do not want you to have to live in those conditions," said Evot.

"Then I suppose we will be leaving," said Raef.

"You will be missed," said Ian.

PART SEVEN

PROMISE ENDS

35

Erif rolled up the scroll he had finished, tied it with grass strands, and wrapped it in skins, tying the skins with leather straps.

"That should protect from moisture," said Erif.

He squeezed the scroll in among the others in the chest, and then shut the lid. It took nearly all his strength to roll the rock in place, closing the chest off inside a pile of boulders.

He walked down off the hill to his camp. As he neared, he heard an unnatural hiss. His right hand flashed to his left hip, pulling his short sword from its scabbard. His left hand pulled the wand of Zul from his belt.

Three Neaverling appeared from behind a rock, black skin still dripping from the sea, needle teeth barred.

"So," said Erif, "more of you have come for what I gave the last of you."

One minion leapt at Erif. Erif stepped back and

extended the wand. A bolt of blue lightning leapt from the stick, turning the beast's nose to ash and lighting the hair on its head on fire. It staggered back, paused a moment, and then ran for the sea.

Another slinked down and struck at Erif's feet, like a viper. Erif brought his sword down, severing its head. Erif stared into the black eyes of the third.

"Shall we play, my little beastie?" said Erif.

The smile faded from Erif's face as three more hissing Neaverling emerged from behind the rocks. All four struck at once.

"Have you seen Luffi?" asked Naan.

"I believe he is in the younglings' room," said Raef. "Shall I fetch him?"

"Yes, please. First meal is ready."

Raef walked across the plank floor to the other end of the house.

"Who would have thought I would live in a house with rooms," said Naan.

Raef smiled at his wife, and then opened the door to the small room where his younglings slept. Luffil was jumping on the down-filled mattress.

"Luffi," said Raef, "it is time for first meal."

Luffil jumped down, pattering bare footed to Raef.

"The bed is softer here," said the youngling, lifting his arms up as he approached Raef.

Raef lifted him to his chest.

"Are we goin' to the market after the first meal?"

"We go to the market every sunrise," said Raef,

"to get bread."

Raef sat his son on the bench next to him, his wife and daughter across the table from him.

"I like it here in Fir Hollow," said Nine. "So many nice people."

"Ana big, big house!" said Luffil.

"Is that ham I smell?" asked Raef.

"Indeed," said Naan, placing a plank with a leg of ham on the center of the table, "and eggs."

Naan spooned eggs from a pan into four of Tren's bowls, passing one to each family member.

"I likes ham!" said Luffil.

"I like Fir Hollow," said Nine. "Are we staying here?"

"We are staying," said Raef, as he pulled his eating knife from his sash and cut a few strips of ham for his son. "We are not travelling like we did with the wagons in summer. We are here to stay."

"Good," said Nine.

"Are you speaking with more Merchants today?" asked Naan.

"I will if I can find any I have not spoken with already," said Raef. "It is a good thing you were able to acquire a commission for a painting. Otherwise we would have no wages at all."

"I am not worried, husband," said Naan. "We have plenty of money left over, even after purchasing this house."

"True," said Raef, "enough to last half a season, but I will need to find a new means of earning a wage eventually."

"You are a wealthy Merchant," said Naan, "I have

every confidence you will."

After first meal Raef walked outside with Nine and Luffil, leaving Naan to work on her painting.

Raef gazed at the fine homes lining the street. He had never been in this part of the Noble Sector, north of the Council Hall when he lived here before. Not even as a Keeper. Only the wealthiest lived here—the highest Nobles and wealthiest Merchants. He marveled at his new home. It was quite large, even for this elite part of the village.

He held Nine's hand as they walked south, passing the Council Hall, entering the village square where the village market took place.

A few Laborers scurried past, headed to the fields to work after giving homage and receiving a blessing at the Ceremonial Lodge. Memories of serving in the Ceremonial Lodge as a young apprentice came to him. Memories of standing with the other Keepers as an adult and proclaiming blessing on the people before they dispersed to their labor.

He shook his head. *I cannot go back to hommage,* he thought, *I do not belong there any more.*

"Can I pay for the bread, Daddy?" asked Nine.

Raef handed his daughter a coin. She brought it to the baker, who smiled and handed her a loaf.

Raef looked among the stalls and booths. There was nothing unusual, nothing that could be purchased in any other village.

What use is it to travel the Province as a Merchant if I have nothing unique to sell? He thought.

After last meal Raef left the younglings with Naan to attend Meditation. Before Promise, he had attended every moon cycle, since he had ten seasons. His own younglings were too small to attend, but Raef wanted to try taking part in the ancient rituals that were once the center of his life.

Raef's stomach tightened as he approached the door of the Ceremonial Lodge. Greenling apprentices lined the entrance, waving fir branches over the heads of those coming to participate. None wore blue robes. None were to become Keepers. Raef lowered his head as the shorter ones strained to lift their branches over him.

Raef sat on a bench in the back of the long room. An apprentice took his arm.

"The front is for Nobles and Merchants," said the greenling.

"I am comfortable here," Raef replied.

The apprentice protested but Raef waved him away. The room filled with villagers, becoming warm from all the bodies. Four Keepers in red robes walked to the front, Raef's father, Folor, Keeper Dimmel, another man Raef did not know, and Prime Keeper Bremmen. The man not known to Raef introduced the meditation. He was young and his voice quivered. Raef smiled, remembering the first ceremonies he had lead. The villagers lifted their faces and closed their eyes.

"He is almost as nervous as you were," came a voice inside Raef's mind.

Raef looked to his left to see the spirit of Zul seated next to him.

Can they see you? Raef thought back.

"Of course not," said the spirit. "Only you can

see or hear me."

Raef looked at the people before him. The lips of some moved silently. Some held hands palm up. Their faces were very earnest.

Here you are, sitting next to me, and they are all beseeching you to reveal yourself to them, Raef thought.

"None of these villagers are seeking me," came Zul's voice, "They try to conjure into existence what they want me to be."

As I did for most of my life, Raef thought back.

"Shall we go?" asked Zul's voice.

Leave? Thought Raef, *Right in the middle of meditation? They will throw me out of the village for committing sacrilege.*

"If we are quiet, they will hardly notice," said Zul's voice.

Raef crept outside and began the walk to his home in the dark, Zul at his side.

"Zul," said Raef aloud, "what are Naan and I to do with ourselves?"

"You appear to be doing fine as you are," said the Great Spirit.

"This is what you healed me to be?" asked Raef. "A wealthy Merchant?"

"Is there anything wrong with that?"

"No," said Raef, "I cannot say that. But…it feels a waste of sorts. You have done so much for us, we have learned so much that others do not understand. It feels like we owe something to the rest of this village, even to the entire Province."

"What are you saying?" asked Zul.

"Naan and I have discussed it," said Raef, "we

want you to use us, in any way you choose. What would you like us to do? We do not have to be wealthy."

"So," said Zul, "I have permission to send you where ever I please?"

"Yes," said Raef.

"That is good to know."

They paused in front of Raef's home.

"What do we do next?" asked Raef.

"Enjoy your family," said the Great Spirit. "Enjoy your house and this time of rest."

The spirit of Zul faded in the moonlight and Raef entered his home.

"The younglings are asleep," said Naan, who was sipping hot tea.

"I will check on them," said Raef.

He entered his younglings' room silently. He stroked Nine's soft hair and smiled down on her. *I will see that she is protected,* Raef told himself. He moved to Luffil's bed. His son was face down on the bed. Raef stroked his son's back.

Enjoy your family, thought Raef, *what did Zul mean by that? Why am I suddenly filled with dread?*

36

Erif read through the scroll in his hand, inspecting it one last time before sealing it in the storage crate.

I can't allow any trace of mold, he thought, *or one bad scroll could spoil the entire lot.*

He worked through each scroll, unfurling each to its full length and scanning the entire surface. He could not help but read the words he had written over the four seasons he had been banished, alone, on the island.

He read of Raef stealing away to meet the dragon as a small youngling. Of Raef becoming an apprentice Keeper before entering his greenling years, trying to impress the Keepers with his work, all the while spending more and more time off in secret with the dragon. He read a passage where Raef took one of his friends to see Rail, making him a co-conspirator to the evil spirit.

Erif saw the passage that described Rail falling from the sky, in the middle of the village, stealing

Raef away and flying him to its lair on the other side of Black Rock. Of Raef spending five seasons in the Great Basin, morphing from a greenling Intercessor to a soulless Dragon Child. Raef entering the seasons of manhood under the captivity of Rail, acting more like a youngling, playing half-naked in the mist and eating regurgitated food from the dragon.

Of Raef's brave return to Fir Hollow and the unfortunate decision of the village to make him their Keeper. There was Raef's marriage to Naan that stood out as a rare spark of hope in his dark life. Raef's betrayal of his apprentice, introducing him to Rail, only for the greenling to be kidnapped by the dragon and taken to Black Rock. Naan's discovery of Raef's friendship with Rail, leading to their leaving all they knew to seek out the Soul Healer in the mountains.

Erif felt wetness slide down his cheek. He tied the final scroll and stowed it in the crate, nailing it shut. The Warrior took a flattened stick, dipped it in a pot of tar that hung over his campfire, and began to seal the crate.

"Brace yourself, my young friend," whispered Erif, "after all you have been through, the next part will be hardest of all."

———·◇·———

"Master Raef!" came a familiar voice from the street outside.

Raef went to the window and saw his old friend, Chaz, dressed in full Warrior garb. Raef put on a coat, for winter was upon them, and went out to greet the man.

"Chaz!" said Raef, clapping his shoulders.

"Raef, my old friend," said Chaz, "I hear you have been in Fir Hollow three moon cycles and still have not come to see me."

Raef smiled, but noticed that Chaz wore despondence behind his smile.

"What is it, Chaz? Is there something I can help you with?"

The Warrior looked to his feet, "Raef, something bad is happening. I do not fully understand, but I am in great fear for you."

"Something bad? Chaz, we are doing well, better than well."

"I was sent word from Summit City that the Chief Magistrate is on his way, along with the Provincial Army."

"To Fir Hollow?"

Chaz looked up, water in his eyes, "He is coming for you, Raef."

"For me?" asked Raef. "Why would the Chief Magistrate want to see me?"

"Not to see you, to put you on trial."

Raef's stomach sank and his blood ran cold.

"Something about Black Rock," Chaz continued, "and people who have disappeared from Fir Hollow."

Raef braced himself, nearly falling from dizziness.

"Raef, I am Chief Detainment Constable in Fir Hollow now," said Chaz, "I received a message from a runner this sunrise to take you into custody. I wanted you to be treated with respect, so I came myself. Raef, I have to arrest you."

Raef looked around him, hoping to see the Great
Spirit. There was only silence.

"I will come," said Raef, "You do not need
restrain me."

At mid sun Raef found himself in a tiny room
built of stone, with walls too tall to climb. A single
square hole two spans up allowed a small amount of
light inside. He had spent very little time in the
Warrior sector and had never even seen the
Confinement Lodge. He found it a truly depressing
place.

"They will take me from my family, Zul," Raef
spoke into the room.

The spirit materialized in front of him.

"I know, Raef," said the ancient being.

"Does this really have to happen?" Raef asked, "I
am no danger to anyone now, I am the opposite!"

"True," said the spirit, "you are not a danger to
villagers any longer."

"They need to know!" said Raef, "They need to
know about Rail. They need to know what is really
happening out in the forest. I smell dragon on half
the village!"

"They do need to know," said Zul. "And you are
the one to tell them."

Raef stared at the spirit, beginning to tremble in
fear. Zul faded from sight. Raef sat on the floor.
There was no furniture. The only thing in the room
was a bucket, Raef assumed to be used as a toilet. He
leaned back against the cold stone wall.

Raef waited, alone, in the cell for two sun's
journeys, hearing nothing of what was to become of

him. Guards came by once a day to throw in a pale of sour pottage, which he had to eat with his hands. Zul did not return, and neither did Chaz. The guards spit at him through the iron-bar door when they happened to pass.

On the third sunrise a guard came and unlocked the door, ordering Raef to come out. He was shackled and led outside by two guards. The sunlight blinded his eyes.

Raef stumbled as he was loaded into a cart and taken to the village square.

Provincial Guards with rainbow feathers sprouting from their helmets surrounded the square. A wooden platform took the center of the square, a tall desk placed upon it. Raef recognized Chief Magistrate, Drumon, sitting behind the desk, as pompous as he had been when he investigated the incident at Moss Rock, so many seasons past.

Raef was pulled roughly from the cart and shoved onto a bench in front of the platform. Raef spotted Chaz from the corner of his eye. His old friend looked truly sad.

Raef dared to gaze around, seeing his father and mother seated to his left. To his surprise, his sister, Mira and her husband Wren were seated with them. They would not look him in the eye. Naan and his younglings were seated nearby, with Keepers Bremen and Dimmel behind her. It seemed every villager in Fir Hollow was also in attendance.

A highly decorated Provincial Guard stepped in front of Magistrate Drumon and the crowd grew silent.

"The Overseers of the Great Province will hereby commence the inquiry," said the Guard.

The Guard stepped aside and Drumon lifted his face.

"You are Raef, son of Folor?" asked Drumon.

"Yes."

"And you grew up in this village of Fir Hollow since birth?"

"Yes."

The man looked down at a scroll in front of him.

"This must be a mistake," said the Magistrate, "for it says you became a Keeper at the age of only ten seasons."

"I was only an apprentice," said Raef, "but that is true."

"An apprentice under whom?" asked Drumon.

Raef's voice caught before he could continue, "Under K...Keeper Dimmel."

"And then you mysteriously vanished for five seasons," said Drumon, "as I learned on my last unfortunate visit to this village. You were supposedly accosted by a spirit in dragon form."

"I had thirteen seasons when I was taken," said Raef, "I returned with eighteen season."

"And where were you all that time?" said Drumon, his eyes growing cold, "A greenling of thirteen seasons, an Intercessor with no training in the hunt, alone in the forest for five seasons, and yet you returned, unharmed."

"I was not alone," said Raef, hanging his head, "Rail took me where it takes everyone it catches—to Black Rock Mountain."

Gasps erupted from all around Raef. One of the Provincial Guards near Drumon turned white. Drumon stared, unflinching, at Raef.

"You lived atop a mountain, through five winters?" asked Drumon, "your story grows more absurd with each telling."

"Not on the mountain," Raef mumbled, "inside it. There is a basin just over the ridge."

"You are full of lies," said Drumon. "No one has even been to the forbidden mountain."

"The entire village saw the beast take me," Raef spoke louder, "it happened in this very spot."

"That is enough!" yelled Drumon. "I will have no more of your fabrications! Your supposed return occurred just before the massacre at Moss Rock. You and this entire village are conspiring against the Provincial Order. I should have you all exterminated."

The crowd buzzed. Drumon waited for silence to continue.

"But I am not here because of Moss Rock," said Drumon, "I am here because of the disappearance of a young greenling called Daz. Can you tell me who Daz was to you?"

"He...was my apprentice," Raef replied.

Raef felt Keeper Dimmel's eyes burning into him. He dare not return the gaze.

"Your apprentice," said Drumon, "and the son of your master, Keeper Dimmel. Odd that after you vanish for so long your own apprentice goes missing."

"I...I took him to see...the dragon," said Raef, staring at the ground.

"I will hear no more of your attempts to divert

your own guilt to some fantastical creature!" growled Drumon. The Magistrate lifted his round stone gavel and pounded it on the square stone beneath it. "You, Raef, are responsible for the disappearance of Daz, son of Dimmel. Do not deny it!"

"I am fully guilty for the disappearance of Daz," said Raef.

The crowd gasped again. Drumon sat back in his chair and folded his arms.

"I do not know what you really did with the greenling," said Drumon, "There are likely other disappearances that you were responsible for. Perhaps you sold them into slavery to a distant province, or you are a murderer. Either way, you are a traitor to this village and the entire Province."

Raef remained silent, his spirit crushed.

"As Chief Magistrate of the Overseers of the Great Province, I hereby declare you guilty of high treason. You deserve death, but I will instead banish you from the Province, so you can do no more harm. Guards, take this pathetic man out of my sight."

One of the warriors lifted Raef roughly by the arm and pushed him back to the cart. Raef stumbled trying to climb in, shaving off the skin of his right shin against the side of the cart. He could not look at his wife or younglings as he was driven back to the Confinement Lodge.

37

Erif began to wrap his long sword in whatever cloth
he had left on the island. After four seasons living
there, not much was left.

Erif's chest grew cold and he paused his work.
He stood slowly looking in all directions. As he
scanned the horizon he froze. In the distance he saw a
dark object in the sky. Erif squinted, the stooped to
unwrap his long sword.

"Zul!" called Erif , "I need you here now!"

Zul appeared at his side. The dark form in the sky
grew nearer, wings now clearly visible.

"The beach," said the Great Spirit.

Erif lowered his eyes to scan the sand. Over a
dozen Neaverling slithered from the sea.

"This is not the place for you to face Rail," said
Zul, "you take the minions."

Erif charged the beach, his long sword held high
over his right shoulder. Lightning cracked from
behind Raef, striking the dragon as it neared the

island.

Four Neaverling were out front, running for Erif. He braced his feet in the sand and swept his sword across, slicing all four across the face and decapitating one. As the three injured beasts staggered in the sand, Erif jumped over them to attack the next three behind him.

The dragon circled above, finally landing in the sand after dodging a second lightning bolt from Zul. Erif turned to watch and saw Zul lift off the ground and flash over the sand to land in front of Rail. A cutting pain in his leg caused Erif to spin back to the minions, ignoring the gash in his leg to defend himself against the attacking teeth and claws.

Flashes of light and explosive sounds told him the spirits were still at war.

Erif stabbed two more minions but noticed the first three he injured seemed to be regaining strength.

How can I fight so many? He wondered.

Erif squatted lower as several beasts circled him, then extended his sword and spun three times as quickly as he could. He felt his sword hit flesh. When he stood, two more dying minions lay in the sand.

One Neaverling jumped, leaping far higher than Erif had expected, then came down over Erif. Erif easily stepped to the side and sliced up and away, eviscerating the creature's bowels.

He continued to thrash his sword in all directions as the remaining minions regrouped and attacked in waves. Erif was aware of a shadow coming closer from behind.

Three Neaverling leapt at him, but burst into

flames as lightning bolts from somewhere behind Erif hit each of them. A shadow loomed overhead; Erif spun around and leapt upward, his long sword extended at arms length. Rail's great head was lowering as Erif's long sword drove into the soft skin behind its chin.

Rail threw its head up as Erif yanked his sword free, falling into the sand. Zul stepped to Erif's side and Erif's ears went deaf as a thunderous bolt shot from the Spirit's hands, blowing the dragon into the sky.

Rail fell, caught its fall with its wings just before hitting the ground, then turned and flew off, its skin smoking and its flight erratic.

Erif still could not hear, but watched Zul vaporize the remaining Neaverling.

Zul helped Erif to his feet. The Warrior shook his head, ears ringing, but his hearing slowly returning. The Spirit collected dune grass and pressed it to the wound on Erif's leg. Erif cried out in brief pain. Then the air grew silent.

"That was close," said Erif. "I am not certain I could do it again."

"There will be no need," said Zul, pointing to the sea. "The boat is approaching."

Erif strained his eyes to the horizon on the left. He could barely make out a sail.

"I…I am going home!" said Erif.

"Yes, you are going home to your family."

Erif began to walk to the surf.

"Erif," said Zul, "the scrolls."

"Ah, yes, the scrolls."

Erif turned to his camp, and then paused.

"They knew the boat was coming," said Erif, "that was their last attempt to destroy the scrolls."

Zul smiled, "Yes, but they failed. The scrolls will make it back to the Great Province."

38

"Now you know," said Raef, sitting back against the stone wall of his cell, nursing a bleeding shin after being kicked by a Provincial Guard.

"I had no idea," said Chaz.

No other guards were present, only Chaz.

"I first visited the dragon when I had only six seasons. A greenling showed me where it hides outside the village."

"I never…no one told me the dragon came near Fir Hollow," said Chaz.

"It visits every village," said Raef, "but always in secret."

Chaz lowered himself to sit next to Raef.

"I am sorry, Raef," said Chaz, "how I treated you when we were young."

"What happened with me and Rail was not your fault, Chaz."

"I have never heard stories like…like what happened to you," said Chaz.

"It happens every sun. There are hundreds of villagers at Black Rock."

"Warriors disappear sometimes too," said Chaz.

"There are plenty of Warriors at Black Rock," said Raef, "though you would no longer recognize them as Warriors."

"I must leave you now," said Chaz, "I will do what I can to help, but I cannot overrule the Overseers."

"I understand."

Raef did not watch Chaz leave. The iron bars closed with a cold clang.

Raef wept for his family. His younglings would grow to greenlings without a father. His wife would live as a widow and be an outcast for marrying a traitor. Banishment often meant death, as the places one was sent were not intended to be survived. Raef was no Warrior; he had not training to survive.

"I do not mind dying," Raef spoke into the air, "but my family does not deserve this. Do you hear me, Zul? Why are you letting this happen?"

The Great Spirit did not make himself known. Raef cried himself to sleep.

Chaz woke Raef before sunrise. Raef saw guards were waiting outside.

"I am not allowed to be your escort," Chaz whispered in Raef's ear. "It is known that I am your friend and the Overseers insist that I not go, for fear I would release you. I have chosen Warriors who are not cruel. It is the most I am able to do."

"I will not forget your kindness," said Raef.

"And I arranged for Naan to come with you as far as possible. They did not like that, but I insisted."

Chaz led Raef outside and handed him over to

two Warriors. Both men appeared near Raef's seasons. Raef was taken to a cart, where Naan already sat. He sat next to her, and then the cart started off, heading south.

"They let me ride along," said Naan, tears in her eyes.

Raef bent over and kissed her. The Warrior guarding him did not try to stop them.

"Where am I to be banished?" Raef asked one of the men.

"To a deserted island off the southern coast," said the Warrior. "The exact location is kept secret."

"And I am to never return," said Raef.

"Your banishment is to be four seasons," said the guard.

Raef felt a ray of hope.

"However," said the second Warrior, who was driving the horses, "no one has every survived a full season of banishment on this island. It is populated with undernourished wolves and sand cats."

Naan began to cry.

"I see," said Raef, "so, a death sentence without having to pronounce a death sentence."

"You will be given supplies," said the first guard, "even a small sword, but I see no hope that you will return."

Raef looked into his wife's eyes, wishing he had words.

"A guard will come by boat every few cycles," the guard continued, "to bring a few supplies and to carry letters."

"And to see if I am still alive," said Raef.

"No use returning, once you no longer are," said the Warrior with a shrug.

The journey took four sun's journeys before they reached Salt Marsh and the southern coast. A barge was waiting, another pair of guards, decidedly less friendly looking, waited on the boat. They gazed out at sea, not bothering to look to see whom their prisoner was.

Raef was helped off the cart and Naan got off with him. One Warrior slung a large pack over Raef's shoulder. With his hands still shackled, Raef had difficulty walking without it slipping off. The Warriors in the cart looked away and did not move to take him to the boat. He turned to the boat and started to walk, Naan at his side. As he stared at the men on the boat, he noted they seemed oddly immobile, still looking out to sea.

"They are not moving at all," said Raef.

"Who?" asked Naan.

"The men on the boat. They look frozen."

"That is because they are," said Zul.

Raef spun to see the Great Spirit behind him. "Zul!" cried Raef.

"They are all, as you say, frozen," said the Spirit.

"You are here to rescue Raef!" cried Naan.

"No, my daughter," said the Sprit, touching her cheek. "I am here to give you each a message."

"Just a message?" asked Raef, "Then why are the guards frozen?"

"I will not allow the Warriors to see me," said Zul. "They are not of mine."

Zul reached into the pack on Raef's shoulder and

pulled out a short sword. Zul stepped behind Raef and took his long hair in his hand, holding it up and slicing his hair off, close to his head.

"You were not born to be an Intercessor," said Zul, "but to be my Warrior."

Raef felt the cold breeze against the skin on his head, a sensation he had never felt.

"I am giving you a new name," Zul continued. "You are to be called Erif from this sun forward, for you are a man of great passion."

Zul dropped Raef's hair into the dust, replaced the sword in the pack.

"And you left this at home," Zul said to Raef, holding a small blue, crystal sphere between his finger and thumb. "You will need it, to remember who you are."

Zul put the stone in Erif's palm, and then turned to Naan.

"My courageous daughter," said the Spirit, "you have done so well. I will be with your husband. No harm will come to him, or to you. You are both protected. Naan, you will from this sun forward be called Tama. Your past will not follow you."

"Zul!" cried Tama.

The Great Spirit slowly faded from sight and the two Warriors on the boat came to life, turning to Erif.

"Who let you out to walk alone?" cried one of the men.

The Warrior leapt from the boat, ran to Raef and roughly shoved him to the water's edge.

"I will wait for you!" called Tama.

The Warrior laughed at Naan as he tossed Erif

onto the barge.

Erif watched his wife waving from the shore as the boat took to the sea. He did not try to stop his tears.

PART EIGHT

THE WARRIOR RETURNS

39

Erif jumped barefoot from the boat into the shallow surf, the breeze bristling his hair. Tama stood at the upper reaches of the sand, her face wrinkled with hardship but wearing a smile of strength. On either side of her were two young ones—Luffil, who had grown to a strapping height that concealed his ten seasons, and Nine, who was nearly a greenlia. His children beamed at him, yet held back with their mother.

Five Provincial Guards stood to one side of Erif's family. The most decorated of them stepped forward, meeting Erif as he came to shore. The guard squinted and looked up at Erif.

"You were not expected to survive," said the guard.

"Have I disappointed you?" smiled Erif.

The four other guards fetched Erif's belongings from the boat. Erif ran to his wife and kissed her. His son and daughter wrapped around them tightly.

"I see you have cut your hair," the lead guard continued, "Do you believe you are a Warrior now, not the Intercessor we banished?"

Two guards carried the sealed chest to shore. Erif turned to watch them, ignoring the Chief.

"Be careful with that," said Erif, "It must not be damaged."

A third guard ran from the boat, carrying a long, cloth-wrapped object.

"Chief!" said the guard, "see what this traitor had with him!"

The Chief unwrapped the long sword Erif had made.

"A sword as long as a man is tall," said the leader.

The Chief took the sword, nearly dropping it. He grunted, struggling before he finally lifted the tip off the sand.

"And what exactly might this weapon be for, traitor?" the Chief asked, "Planning to do still more damage among us?"

"It is not meant for men," Erif replied.

The five Provincial Guards circled Erif and his family. Erif pulled a blue, circular stone from a pouch at his sash and held it up so that the sun shone through it.

"I know who I am," Erif replied, "and I am a Warrior. And the long sword you hold is to fight dragons."

HOW TO HELP THE AUTHOR

If you enjoyed reading Raef's adventure in *Under the Burning Sun*, your rating would be highly appreciated. Just go to your favorite bookseller and leave a review —even a single sentence will help!

Thank you!

John W Fort

ABOUT THE AUTHOR

John W Fort was born in Texas, moved to the Pacific Northwest as a child, and lived for two years in Brazil in his twenties. He has a love for the outdoors, music, and old cars which he pursues when not writing.

Diagnosed as hyperactive and attention deficit as a child he chooses to embrace the oddity and mental frenzy it provides rather than seek a cure. John loves deep spirited conversation, but only in person, having a general disdain for social media.

He lives with his wife and two children in Oregon.

ABOUT THE FORBIDDEN SCROLLS

The Forbidden Scrolls is a chronicle of secrets a society does not want to admit to and topics they would rather ignore. As we see secrets and taboo subjects only harm those enforcing them.

Set in the medieval time period of the fictional world, The Great Province, a banished warrior, Erif, records his visions of a young boy, Raef, growing up and trying to make sense of the secrets and lies his village keeps. Everything Erif writes is forbidden but he is determined to complete his record of the visions and return the scrolls to The Great Province to confront them with their lies.

The Forbidden Scrolls include:

Book 1: The Shadow of Black Rock
Book 2: The Other Side of Black Rock
Book 3: Under the Burning Sun

The series will continue...

29055134R00168

Made in the USA
San Bernardino, CA
12 March 2019